Mr. Montessori and
beach to discover th
contemporary, it's nc
faintly of damp.

Its appearance and origins are a mystery. A joke? An inverted theft? A break in the fabric of reality? Yes, the police take the "crime" seriously. But what happens next lies outside their expertise. Strange sounds in the night. A half-bathroom toilet with a mind of its own. Odd, fleeting glimpses of something (or someone) in mirrors. The inexplicable vision of Montessori's neighbor: He swears he saw a burglar. . . .

Montessori's quest for answers will take him to a dank highway overpass in decayed upstate New York, a very strange dry-cleaning supply concern in outermost Queens, and into the depths of an eerie, warped forest where time and space no longer connect, all while putting his ever-more-troubled marriage and young family in grave danger. But that's what it costs to find out if we own our possessions — or if they own us.

Munson emerges as a master stylist in this tense, taut work of surreal humor and psychological horror.

SAM MUNSON is the author of *Dog Symphony* (New Directions), *The War Against the Assholes* (Saga), and *The November Criminals* (Doubleday). His fiction has appeared in *Granta*, *Guernica*, *McSweeney's*, *n+1*, *Tablet*, and elsewhere.

Also by Sam Munson

Dog Symphony

The War Against the Assholes

The November Criminals

For Rebecca, Felix, and Anouk

The SOFA

SAM MUNSON

Two Dollar Radio
Books too loud to ignore

Two Dollar Radio
Books too loud to Ignore

WHO WE ARE TWO DOLLAR RADIO is a family-run outfit dedicated to reaffirming the cultural and artistic spirit of the publishing industry. We aim to do this by presenting bold works of literary merit, each book, individually and collectively, providing a sonic progression that we believe to be too loud to ignore.

TwoDollarRadio.com

Proudly based in
Columbus
OHIO

@TwoDollarRadio

@TwoDollarRadio

/TwoDollarRadio

Love the
PLANET?
So do we.

Printed on Rolland Enviro. This paper contains 100% post-consumer fiber, is manufactured using renewable energy - Biogas and processed chlorine free.

Printed in Canada

 100%

PCF

BIO GAS ENERGY

∞ PERMANENT

SOME RECOMMENDED LOCATIONS FOR READING:
In a theater waiting for a movie to start, at the food court in the mall, on a bench in Villa Borghese, or pretty much anywhere because books are portable and the perfect technology!

AUTHOR PHOTO →
Anouk Munson

COVER DESIGN →
Eric Obenauf

Two Dollar Radio would like to acknowledge that the land where we live and work is the contemporary territory of multiple Indigenous Nations.

"Let's just saw each other in half and call it a night."

— Jerry Seinfeld

The SOFA

The truck pulled ahead of Montessori as he was driving home from the beach. It said HERAKLITOS MOVERS. The truck was tall and wide enough that it interfered with Montessori's vision of the road ahead.

He said: They should make a law, trucks like this are impossible.

His older son said: At least if we get in an accident it won't be our fault, we can blame the truck.

His younger son laughed at this, and even Montessori chuckled although he was very tired from swimming and sitting in the sun.

The moving truck was not going slowly or driving erratically. It moved at a high, constant speed, dead straight in its lane. The driving impressed Montessori. More and more trucks these days swayed and weaved around as they drove. The truck also, he had to be honest, did make driving easier in one way. Before, the sun had been shining almost directly into Montessori's eyes. So strongly that his sunglasses had no effect and he still had to squint to see. Now? He was able to appreciate the sky and cool breeze a little more. The truck was not even pumping out bad-smelling exhaust. Must be one of the new models.

The truck stayed in front of them long after the signs for their exit began to appear. To Montessori's mild surprise, it pulled off onto their exit ahead of them.

His younger son said: Look – it's going the same direction we are.

His older son said: Don't be stupid, it's just chance. Right, dad?

Montessori said: I think it's probably a coincidence, but then again you never know.

His wife said: I think it's going the same direction as we are. And I think that's good because it's keeping the front seat nice and shady.

It should be noted here that this Montessori, our Montessori, was related neither to the hygienic hangman who shared his name nor to the famous "inventor of kindergarten." He smiled the smile of just such a non-related man as he listened to his wife and children talking about the truck, fate, and shade from the sun. Their voices mixing with the cool breeze and the sky getting redder. They stopped for a long dinner at a restaurant, as they always did after going to the beach. His sons were excited and happy; his wife leaned against Montessori's arm and drowsed a little in the booth. By the time they left, it was dark. The green-black darkness that falls in the summer. You know all about it.

There was more traffic, quite bad traffic, for the rest of the drive. When they got back home, their house was cool and dark. Montessori did not bother turning on the lights downstairs in the living room or dining room. He opened a can of food for their cat, Old Abel, who chirped and whisked around Montessori's legs. Everyone trotted up to their bedrooms, called out blurry goodnights. Mrs. Montessori undressed, moonlight shining on her skin and underwear, and lay down. Soon she snored with incredible, rasping deep draughts.

Despite the late night, Montessori woke up early. He always did in the summer. He and his wife liked to keep the curtains and (weather permitting) windows open. In the warm months this meant light and bird sounds woke them usually before six. The air was even cooler, even sweeter than it had been last night. An irregular breeze moved the pushed-aside curtains and the green dress Mrs. Montessori had hung over the armchair before climbing into bed. Montessori lay there, listening. His wife was still snoring, just more softly and evenly.

Finally, the need to piss got him up. As he was pulling on a shirt, his younger son ran into the room.

Montessori lifted a finger to his lips. The noise had failed to wake up his wife. His son was still trying to speak, so Montessori walked him out into the hall. The boy was moving in the hopping, desperate way of children with news.

He said: What's the matter.

His younger son said: Come, just come.

He raced off downstairs. Montessori wondered what the boy wanted to show him. There was a woodpecker that lived in the oak across the street. Perhaps it was pecking away. There might be a snail on the window, or simply the dew on the grass in their small front yard.

In the living room, his son stood and pointed at the sofa. For a while, Montessori wondered what on earth he was supposed to be looking at.

Then he realized: The sofa was different.

Their sofa, their actual sofa, was wide and deep, upholstered in dark fabric. Long enough for Montessori to stretch out on and have room at head and feet (and he was fairly tall), and set low to the ground. This sofa was narrow and shallow, high up on tall, yellow legs with volute feet, and covered with a yellow-green striped fabric. Two doilies, faded lace, covered each of the lumpy, vestigial headrests rising up from the back. Nothing else in the room was different. Nothing had been disturbed. Montessori squatted down to examine the sofa. The fabric was imitation velvet; his hand left marks in its nap. The legs were wood; the paint was thickly applied and a little greasy. The warped cushions gave off a slight, damp smell.

His younger son stood nearby, eyes wide and lips trembling. Montessori said: It's OK, someone is just playing a joke on us.

His son said: Why would they do that? I liked the old sofa.

Montessori went and checked the doors and windows. Front door locked, kitchen door locked, basement door locked, all first-floor windows locked. There were no signs of forced entry (a phrase Montessori knew well, from movies and TV) and no damage to the window or doorframes or floors to suggest the sofa had been shoved through. There was no sign, none, of the old sofa. That was equally mysterious, as it was almost twice as big.

Mrs. Montessori came down. She was yawning.

Her younger son said: Mom, we have kind of a disaster here.

When she saw the sofa, she said: What is this? What's going on?

Montessori said: It's some stupid prank. I am going to call the cops.

By now his older son (named Josep, in fact) had woken up and also come downstairs. He did not even notice the sofa until his younger brother pointed it out to him, and then he too approached it, examined it. He lifted up the cushions, which Montessori had not thought to do. Under the left cushion was a yellowed, oblong slip stitched into the upholstery seam.

Josep read the one word printed on it aloud: MEERVERMESSER.

This odd word Montessori had never heard before. It must be the name of the sofa's owner. Or one of its previous owners. Presumably not the one responsible for the prank, given the obvious age of the slip. It crumbled a little between Montessori's fingers. He tugged it free, put it in an envelope and then called the police.

An officer came quite quickly. He was young, a little fat, totally bald when he took off his cap. As Montessori explained, his eyes widened and he began to smile.

He said: That's the first time I've ever heard of anyone doing anything like this. What was the value of the item that was stolen?

His smile reassured Montessori and Mrs. Montessori. The boys too. They went to the park to play soccer, while Montessori looked up the precise cost of the missing couch and Mrs. Montessori gave the other information for the police report. The officer, when he had taken it all down, promised to find out everything he could and keep them updated.

He said: In the meantime, at least you still have a sofa!

Montessori knew he could not expect much more. After all, nothing had been damaged, no violence committed. The thief had even left a sofa in exchange. Still: he had hoped the officer might be more helpful. He could tell from his wife's face that she was a little disappointed too.

Not least because, when he went to order a new couch, he found that the model and color they had were on back order. It would be three weeks until an exact replacement arrived. There were other couches available sooner, but Mrs. Montessori disliked them all (and Montessori was not crazy about them either). There was no point in going down to the store itself: all its stock was available online. Other furniture purveyors they did not like; everything they had bought from them always fell apart after a year or so. Montessori brought down from the attic the woven, red and gold blankets he had bought years ago in Morocco and draped them over the sofa, while Mrs. Montessori dug up some throw pillows and put them on top. There was less room to sit, but now the sofa at least looked better. It's odd, stale smell was getting fainter and fainter with each passing moment (it seemed).

The boys, after they got back from soccer, said they liked the new sofa more with the blankets and pillows on it. By the end of the day, its presence was almost normal. The main thing was that Montessori could no longer stretch out on it full-length and that the cushions were stiffer and a little less comfortable. The other main problem was with Old Abel. He refused to climb up on the sofa, even when they enticed him with food, with the blankets and pillows.

When Montessori checked in with the police officer – he had given his name and direct phone number – the answer was always the same. Nothing yet, and frankly don't be too hopeful. This made sense. The crime, after all, was bizarre. Possibly not criminal. He did not want to annoy the officer, who was so polite and accommodating, so he did not check in very often. Soon enough he stopped doing it at all. The story of the new sofa, the temporary sofa, they told their neighbors and friends. Because Montessori and Mrs. Montessori smiled while they told it, their neighbors and friends smiled too.

With one exception. That was old Señor Periander, who lived down in the adjoining house (the Montessori's home was a row house, but an end one, so it only shared a single wall). Montessori told the old man about it.

He said: It's none of my business but you should be more concerned.

Montessori said: I don't see why, they didn't really do us any harm.

The old man said: They took your sofa and gave you a shitty one. If that's not harm I don't know what is.

To Montessori's surprise, the old man was angry. The fatty, swinging skin under his neck was a little pink and his eyes had gone pink too. He had raised his voice, his hands.

Montessori said: I guess we'll just have to disagree.

The old man shrugged and went back to watering the small, square front lawn.

The strange name – MEERVERMESSER – also led Montessori nowhere. He looked it up on the internet and found only a defunct dry-cleaning supply company with the name J. MEERVERMESSER & ASSOC, with an address in the Bronx. Nothing else, not even in Germany or Switzerland. Maybe it belonged to some sort of Jew whose entire line had been wiped out. Or who knows – a Nazi who died in the hot jungles of Brazil? Both possibilities stimulated Montessori's imagination, and he found his mind drifting a little whenever he sat down on the sofa. After all, its immediately previous owner had cared enough to keep it in good shape (apart from the smell) despite its obvious age. The nonexistent Meervermesser himself had taken the time to sew his name into it. Yes, this sofa represented a triumph of burgherish probity and patience. No wonder Montessori daydreamed.

About a week before the new couch was due to arrive, Montessori got a call from the manufacturer. They were very sorry, but an unforeseeable delay had arisen. The couch was not ready now and would not be ready in time. Montessori now had a choice: an immediate full refund or a voucher to spend on another couch for twice as much.

Montessori said: And what if I don't want a different couch – how long will the wait be?

The manufacturer's representative said: Sir, it will be a long time. We don't exactly know.

Montessori said: Do I have to decide right now?

The manufacturer's representative said: No, not at all. Call us when you've made up your mind, and we apologize again.

Montessori and his wife discussed the problem that night. There were not really any other couches they wanted, either from that manufacturer or any other. On the other hand, giving up the chance of getting all the money back seemed silly. They went to bed without deciding anything. In the morning, they talked it over again and decided to wait. It would be annoying, but getting a refund was pointless since they only wanted that couch, and they had a perfectly usable replacement (left by the thief) to use in the meantime.

When Montessori called to tell the company of his decision, the manufacturer's representative sounded flustered.

She said: Are you sure?

Montessori said: Yes, we are.

She said: If you change your mind let us know. It's going to be a while, sir.

Montessori found his wife staring at the sofa when he got off the phone. She started rearranging the blankets, massaging the pillows. She finished. Montessori could not tell the difference. He still knew there was one, however. Otherwise she would not have been smiling so broadly.

Because he had not spoken to the officer in a while, Montessori left a message for him at the precinct that night. Nothing angry, just checking in. The officer usually took a few days to call back. Again, Montessori understood. In the hierarchy of crime, this event ranked low. (Had he been related to the hygienic hangman who shared his name, he might have felt differently.) So he did not think more about the call the next day, and when his assistant told him the police were on the phone for him, he found he was happily surprised.

The voice on the phone was different, however: a woman.

She said: Is this Mr. Montessori?

Montessori said: Yes – is there any news?

The officer said: And your address is XXXXXXXXXX?

Montessori said: It is.

The officer said: I wanted to let you know one of your neighbors reported someone was burglarizing your house. Would it
be possible for you or any other authorized person to come and
speak with us?

When Montessori got home – he only stopped to text his wife
– he found a small crowd in front of the house he had left that
morning. He saw two police officers he did not recognize and
old Señor Periander, who was waving his arms and yelling.

He yelled: Don't act like you don't know what I mean!

The officer (the taller one) said: Calm down, sir, no one is acting
like anything.

Montessori said: What happened?

It turned out that the old man had seen someone in the upstairs
window. A figure he did not recognize. Male, pale, fat, with
a mustache (Montessori was clean-shaven and in good shape
for a man his age). Señor Periander knew both Montessori
and his wife and Josep and his brother were out, so he had –
like any good neighbor – called the police. The officers, after
they arrived, found no sign of a break in anywhere. So they
had called Montessori, to avoid breaking down his door. Would

he unlock it for them? Montessori let the two officers in, while Señor Periander looked at him. After a few minutes the shorter officer came back out.

She said: It's safe to go in. (This was the woman who had called him.)

The taller officer escorted Montessori around the house, while the officer who had called him stayed by the door to stop Señor Periander from entering. Montessori found nothing disarranged or changed, even the blankets and pillows on the sofa were in the same position. He checked the desk drawer where he and his wife kept passports, bank documents, and other valuable papers. All there. Their emergency supply of cash, in a locked metal box in the closet, was still there, as was all his wife's jewelry and his cufflinks. Both their computers and their sons', his older son's phone. No silverware was missing (though they only had stainless steel). There was nothing much else of obvious value in the house. Nothing was broken, no windows or locks, no sill or jamb showed signs of having been jimmied or forced – just like the police said. After the officers left – Señor Periander shook his head, as if in exasperation, and trudged back to his own house – Montessori checked everything again. Just to be sure. He found nothing. He texted his wife again to let her know there had not been a break-in, and then he returned to his office. He realized on the way there that in his excitement he had forgotten to ask the two officers for further news of his sofa.

That night, he and his wife both checked the windows and doors, and Montessori even went and sat out in the backyard until it was late. Not because he was frightened, but because he wanted to see if some trick of the light might have been responsible for what Señor Periander had seen. The air was still, cool-warm. The smell of the cut grass from Señor Periander's back lawn rose up. Montessori remembered he needed to cut his own grass. A flicker of movement in a window caught his eye. He looked at it head on and saw it was a curtain moving: back and forth, jerky, mechanical. He knew at once it was Old Abel clawing at it, from below the window, and soon enough the cat appeared and sat on the sill, staring out at Montessori with his eyes, amber and a little phosphorescent. That must have been what Señor Periander had seen. It really did look, when caught in your peripheral vision, like someone passing through the room.

Nonetheless, that night Montessori found he was being wakened from sleep by noises. They made him come awake with a violent, physical convulsion. He had heard something, he knew it. As he listened, he would hear it again. Old Abel leaping down or leaping up, the slight ticking sounds that all old houses make. It had seemed much louder in his drowsing state, loud and right near his ear. His wakings did not disturb his wife, who went on snoring lightly. Eventually, near dawn, Montessori gave up. He checked on both his sons, as he had done when they were much younger. Both asleep, Josep with his mouth wide open (like his mother). He went downstairs. The kitchen was cool and silent. The smell of the coffee he brewed mixed with the smell of the grass, still lingering, and the rising smell of asphalt. As usual, he needed to piss. When he went to the bathroom off the kitchen, he found the door locked.

This had happened before. Sometimes one of the boys left the lock depressed and then shut the door behind them when they left. Sometimes the spring engaged on its own. There was a pinhole you could thread a straightened paper clip through to release it, and they kept such a paper clip in the silverware drawer for that purpose. As Montessori kneeled down to insert it, the toilet flushed.

He paused in confusion. He had just seen everyone else in their beds. As he hesitated, he heard the hissing sound of the sink faucet.

Fuck, Señor Periander had been right! Somehow, the old man had been right. Montessori suppressed his cry and grabbed a butcher knife from the wooden block on the kitchen counter near the sink. He positioned himself outside the door. He stood there for a long time. No one came out. The water was still running. He began to feel foolish. He came closer to the door.

He called out: Hello?

No response. But if it was some housebreaker, why would he answer? On the other hand, why break into someone's house to take a piss or a shit and wash up afterward? Montessori put the knife down and used the paperclip to pop open the lock, pressing all his weight against the door to prevent the housebreaker from leaving.

He said: I am going to call the police.

Still no answer. The water was hissing. Montessori pulled open the door. The bathroom was empty. The toilet was hissing, not the sink. Just the regular hiss as the tank filled back up. Montessori found he was breathing hard and fast. He put the knife back in the block and sat staring into the bathroom from a seat in the kitchen. The toilet stopped hissing. His breathing and heart slowed down. Yet it had been the faucet, it had. He knew the difference between the sounds. The faucet was louder and more melodic; the toilet hiss had a longer, more elegant periodicity. Still – no water! He could see it, right there! And that toilet did flush on its own sometimes, any toilet was capable of that.

By the time his wife and younger son had come down, Montessori had managed to assure himself that he had made a mistake. That his own senses had misled him. He said nothing about it to his wife or his younger son (or Josep, once the boy had woken up). After they had all left, his wife to her office and the boys for school, Montessori went through the house one more time. Starting in the attic, finishing in the basement. He knew it was foolish and empty but he did it anyway. He opened every closet and checked inside; he examined all the window latches. He even moved the boxes out of the small room they used for storage in the basement. There was a tiny alcove in the east wall, just big enough for a crouching man. No one there, as he knew would be the case. He spent a long time in the shower, cleaning dust from his hair, ears and hands, and grinning a little at his own nervous stupidity. He spent his spare time at his own office that day trying to find more people with the name Meervermesser. His first search might have missed something; he had not tried criminal complaints, bankruptcies, arrests, births, deaths. Anything like that. He found nothing. That was unusual. Most names found their way into the courts. Almost on their own. (And perhaps your own name is crawling around like an insect, right now). Still, it bothered him less than he thought it would. In fact, it made him feel better.

One of the junior assessors had fucked up an evaluation, and Montessori had to spend more than two hours going through it with him to fix it. As a result, he got home late. It was already dark. He saw, once more, a patrol car in front of his house, all the lights on inside. He found the first cop in the living room with his wife. He was sitting in the armchair, she on the new sofa. She looked relaxed, a little sad, which made Montessori feel better.

Mrs. Montessori said: We've gotten some bad news.

The officer said: Yes, I was just saying. We found your couch, Mr. Montessori. And it was in terrible shape.

He explained that a colleague of his had found it under a bridge. He showed Montessori, and Mrs. Montessori, photos of the crime scene. The bridge itself was made of stone. A large green sign was affixed to it, with a road name he did not know. HARRISON MEMORIAL PKWY. Under the bridge, a thick sheaf of blue shade and a filthy, stony strand. The river flowing brown and foamy. The sofa itself: torn up, white-yellow flashes of stuffing. Cushions missing, one cut in half, and the canvas covering the box of the base ripped apart to reveal the springs. A few had been pulled into near straightness, and they stuck up from the couch like plant fronds. Montessori felt sick. Nauseated. As if he were looking at a corpse. That thought made him chuckle. He saw his wife was smiling as well.

The officer said: I don't see what's so funny, Mr. Montessori. Burglary is a serious crime. And if I recall you were quite upset when it happened.

He was frowning. That made sense. It probably seemed like Montessori and Mrs. Montessori were making fun of his job. He assumed a more serious expression and handed the phone back. He could see, in the corner of his eye, that his wife was also forcing her face to be calm. Once the cop was gone, Montessori and his wife found they could not stop chuckling about it. Yes, it was lonely, even sad. Yes, it had made them sick (Montessori found out his wife had also been nauseated). But to present it as though it were a human body…

Mrs. Montessori said: Imagine if that were your job, to announce the deaths of furniture!

The boys thought it was funny as well. They had been at a friends' house when the cop came so they did not hear about it until the next day. Josep laughed the hardest and Montessori's younger son followed (though his eyes were wide as if with mild fear). Josep even made jokes about the "dead couch" or "our dearly departed couch." He started patting the new sofa with affection. After all, they'd better get used to it! Montessori's younger son imitated Josep's patting as well, with gentle, lovely strokes.

The boys had been much kinder to the new sofa than Montessori would have imagined. The old couch they hurled themselves on; his younger son used it as a springboard. The new sofa they treated with the same respect they showed their grandparents (that was the only analogy that Montessori could come up with, and he also knew it was not a good one). The patting – and the *goodnights* that his younger son soon added to the patting – Mrs. Montessori said she found very encouraging. Montessori agreed, but also thought that it seemed out of character, for Josep at least. He had never paid any real attention to the furniture in their house before. Montessori could hardly complain. It was good to see a little courtly behavior in the boys, he thought, and it clearly made his wife happy. So he kept silent about it. As he had kept silent about the faucet sound in the bathroom.

Whenever he found himself awake early, he sat with his coffee in a kitchen chair. There, he had a direct line of sight to the bathroom door. He had not heard the faucet noise again, though twice the toilet flushed itself. Even though that had happened many times before, he now darted in each time. No one there. He always made sure to shit and piss in that bathroom whenever he could. He examined the faucet and toilet himself, and nothing was out of order. He did not want to call in a plumber. How could he even explain what the problem was?

He checked the house, too, as he had done the first time. Once everyone else had gone to bed, he would climb the stairs to the attic and scan the room, the small storage closets, open the wooden panels that hid the ductwork, check the living room, kitchen, dining room, and basement. He had rearranged the box-storage room for easier access. After that? Up the yard stairs to take a walk around.

Señor Periander was often out back, and the sweet, abrasive smell from his cigar would drift over along with the dissipating blue smoke. He said nothing. He had not spoken to Montessori since the police visited him. He would not look at Montessori, staring off into the green-black instead. Just as he had the first time, Montessori never found anything. One night he came back to bed to find his wife awake. She was shivering a little, though the night was warm.

Montessori said: Are you getting sick?

Mrs. Montessori said: No, I just feel cold.

His wife reached out. He held her for a while. She was shivering, really shivering. In the next room Montessori heard Josep snoring. His snores sounded just like his mother's.

Mrs. Montessori said: Why do you always get up and go downstairs? And into the yard?

Montessori said: I don't really know. Just being superstitious, I guess.

They lay next to each other, holding hands. For once, Montessori realized, he was going to fall asleep before she did. She was still up, still shivering, as his eyes closed.

The scream woke him up. It was dark and his vision was blurry. Mrs. Montessori sat upright and still. The scream came from their younger son. As Montessori ran down the hall, he heard Josep still snoring. His younger son was pressed hard against the headboard of his bed. His eyes were open and so was his mouth. He was screaming and screaming, drawn-out and word-less. He kept doing it when Montessori turned on the light. From the glazed look in his eyes, Montessori could tell his son was still asleep.

He put his mouth right to the boy's ear and said: It's me, I'm right here, you're asleep and you're having a dream.

His younger son said: I know, I know.

Montessori said: It's a dream, I'm right here, you're asleep.

His younger son said: I know, I know I'm asleep.

Then he went stock still and started to shiver, like his mother had. His body stiff, as though he was going to stand up, to leap up and start running. For a moment, Montessori was frightened to the point of nausea. The boy relaxed, almost right away, and started breathing deep and evenly. His eyes peacefully shut and his limbs warmly, softly slack. Montessori laid him back down, covered him, ran a hand down the curve of his cheek. He turned off the light and sat in the boy's desk chair, watching and listen-ing to him sleep, until he felt his own eyes closing again.

While they were eating breakfast the next morning, Montessori asked him: What were you dreaming about?

His younger son said: Wow, I had a dream? I didn't even remember!

Josep said: I never have any dreams, it's not fair.

The sofa no longer smelled damp or stale at all. It had taken on the familiar smell of the house, which to Montessori smelled like coffee and hand soap. His wife even suggested they clean the upholstery, since it seemed like it might be there for a while. Montessori said it was foolish to spend the money. After all, it had been a free replacement. No need to invest in it. What he really wanted to know, and knew he would never discover, was how the thieves had gotten the original couch out of the house. It had required two men to move it in, and they had made a lot of noise. It was possible he and his family were so tired out from the beach they'd slept through it. That didn't seem likely, even though he knew it was the only possible solution.

He pondered this question anew every time he found himself alone in the kitchen. Not only because of the bathroom, but because his younger son had made a drawing of the couch, the old couch, and his wife had taped it up on the refrigerator. His son had a sure, adult hand when he drew, and the couch he had reproduced not faithfully but precisely. The color he had used a pencil to shade in. Above it, in large, neat, bending letters, he had written RIP COUCH. Josep and Mrs. Montessori had been delighted by the drawing. Montessori too. It brought to mind the theft every time he saw it. The theft and the vandalism done to the first couch.

Whenever he called the furniture store, they told him the same thing. There were still big problems with manufacturing and delivery due to supply chain stresses, and those logistical issues would persist for some time. A firm delivery date for the couch they could not supply. They did not know when they might be able to give him even that. The sales rep always repeated the offer of a refund, explaining that it would be good until

48 hours before the new couch went into production, and they would inform him at least a week before that happened. For the moment, their manufacturing troubles had no end in sight. The sales reps were so calm and patient that Montessori felt none of his usual anger when dealing with such situations. As Mrs. Montessori pointed out, they did have a sofa. It's not as though there was nowhere to sit (even if it was smaller).

Still, he asked some of his colleagues about other furniture options. They all used places he and Mrs. Montessori disliked. (Indeed, they all used the same shop: Harvard & Marrow.) So their recommendations were useless. He decided he would start looking for used couches, i.e. "antiques." Even though the one they had now was a clear antique. His wife agreed that they might have better luck. Every time they went to the shop – they left the boys at home, with Josep in charge – no matter how long they spent looking they could find nothing. Either the shop had only armchairs and rockers, or the couches they had were even smaller and more rickety than the replacement. Mrs. Montessori, after one such outing, asked the store owner if she knew any good upholsterers who worked on older pieces. They had a sofa at home that they were thinking of replacing, but refurbishing it was also an option. The woman claimed she did not, which Montessori suspected as an obvious lie. She was simply angry they had not bought anything. The whole problem seemed absurd, even sinister, to Montessori. How on earth could it be so difficult to purchase a couch? They had standards, yes, but not unreasonable ones. Where did these insane obstacles come from? And you know them too, don't lie…

His wife thought he was overreacting. Montessori knew the opposite was true. He was being overly restrained. Every time they walked into an antique shop now – they had started going farther and farther afield, to places that imported Danish and other Nordic furniture in bulk – he felt an urge toward actual violence against the helpless furniture. Each piece wore the congested, congenitally moronic expression common to Northern Europeans. The store owners, even though they were simply Americans (just like Mr. and Mrs. Montessori) displayed the same characteristics. They followed Montessori and his wife around their airless shops with their phlegmy gazes. No matter how clear and basic the questions they asked, the shop owners and employees responded with dull arrogance. Montessori, or Mrs. Montessori, had to repeat and repeat themselves to the insulting silences of these clerks and owners.

That's why, after a while, the upholstery concept took firmer root. They began visiting specialized fabric stores as well. Here Mr. Montessori felt much calmer. The owners were not Nordic and pseudo-Nordic imbeciles, they did not breathe with their wide mouths open. They were helpful and efficient. Montessori also enjoyed physically being among the different fabrics, and when neither his wife nor the sales assistant was looking would smell them, test the nap and softness with his hairy cheek. They managed to decide on a fabric relatively quickly: a dark gray, close-woven one that almost matched the covering of the dead couch. It would be far less expensive, they discovered, to purchase the fabric and have the old sofa re-covered than to buy a new one. The fabric store was happy to recommend a good upholsterer; his rates were extremely reasonable. Mrs. Montessori made the arrangements with a big smile. Montessori found he was grinning too. He called the upholsterer while they were driving home, and it turned out the man was available the following week. Once Montessori explained the job, he said it would take only one day, and he would even do it in their house to save them from having to transport the couch to his workshop (assuming they did not mind the mess). He made the appointment right then, as his wife lifted one hand from the steering wheel to give a thumbs up.

The boys were at the park – Josep had texted – so the house was empty and quiet when they got back. Filled with the cool, still absence of humans. They cleared all the blankets off the sofa and Montessori took photographs with his phone. The upholsterer had asked for front, rear, top, both sides and bottom so that he could begin planning out his work. Montessori had finished and found his wife in the kitchen staring at the refrigerator.

She said: Hey, he drew a little guy. Next to the couch.

She was right. Added to the lithe drawing of the dead couch his younger son had made was a human figure, leaning jauntily on his elbow on the armrest. The proportions were basically correct, as was the posture – again Montessori marveled at his younger son's skill. The face plump and somehow jolly, but not smiling. Round glasses, round cheeks, round mustache.

Montessori said: It looks like Groucho Marx.

Mrs. Montessori said: I think it looks more like Charlie Chaplin.

When the boys got back, Montessori asked his younger son about the drawing. His younger son looked blank.

He said: I didn't do that. I was done with the drawing.

Josep said: Oh come on, of course you did! And you're not in trouble!

His younger son said: I didn't! I didn't!

Josep said: It's really good, I like that little guy.

Montessori's younger son said: I don't know who it is and I didn't draw it.

Mrs. Montessori said: I know who did – must be Mr. Meervermesser, right?

Their younger son looked at Mrs. Montessori, eyes wide. He wrung his hands together. Josep put an arm around his shoulders.

Mrs. Montessori said: I was kidding. I was kidding. OK?

Their younger son nodded. He wiped at his eyes with the back of his hand and ran off upstairs to his room without another word.

His younger son had spoken with the weary fluency of an adult (he often did). He probably believed, Montessori thought, that once a drawing was up on the fridge it assumed museum status and further changes were a kind of vandalism. Mrs. Montessori and Josep avoided mentioning the drawing. Their younger son also said nothing about it, though Montessori noticed the boy often glanced at the added figure, or touched it. Even put his eyes close to the paper, less than an inch away, and stared. He also adjusted it neatly on the fridge itself. If it had slipped or one of the magnets had come loose from a corner, he corrected it. This happened more frequently than Montessori would have thought. He found out why, quite by chance. Old Abel, too, was interested in the drawing. He would crouch at the base of the fridge and leap up and bat at it, slapping it until it started to hang or flap, until a corner had worked its way out from under the magnet. Montessori put the drawing as high up as there was room for it, near the top edge of the door. Old Abel still managed to get it loose, and soon the paper's lower edge started to become ragged. Montessori found that the little figure often drew his eye as well, especially when he was having his morning coffee in the kitchen (he did so every day now). His younger son must have drawn it, there was no other explanation despite his denials.

The following Monday, Montessori went out of town. Not far, just upstate. Montessori was going to speak with a company's executive committee about their transaction project with Montessori's firm. As always when leaving on work travel, he felt mildly guilty, although he knew his employees would handle everything irreproachably in his brief absence. The morning he left he stood in front of the fridge as he drank his coffee. He wanted to get rid of the drawing. Who knew how the boy would react? And to take that chance right as he was leaving seemed unfair to his wife, who was also slated for a busy day. He ended up leaving it as it was. He thought about the drawing, about the little figure, the whole drive. He had almost reached the firm's office campus when he realized he needed some gas. He found a station and pulled in, and as he was filling the tank and looking idly around, he saw on the other side of the wide highway a stone bridge over the dirty river he had been driving along. The bridge reminded him of something. He did not know what, until he saw the green road sign affixed to it: HARRISON MEMORIAL PKWY.

He overfilled the tank a little. The vacuous, royal smell of the splashed gas rose up. It would take no time to get there, and he had more than two hours. The meeting was at eleven. Montessori, after driving around for a while, found a stone plaza next to the river about a hundred yards upstream from the bridge, with parking spaces. A "nature point," it said on the small signs on poles sticking up from the grassy dirt (stinking of piss). He parked and began to pick his way along the stony bank toward the blue shadow under the arching bridge. He felt absurd for the first minute of his journey, then he began to feel fine about it and even walked faster and whistled. It was a warm day. As soon as he walked under the bridge he was cold. The shade was dense and the bridge stones gave off cold. The noise of the river was louder, doubled and redoubled, confused and woven. The piss smell was stronger, and he smelled shit too. His eyes had to adjust to the dimness. Then he saw it. The dead couch. It was sitting there, just as it had been in the photo the cop had shown him. As he got closer, he saw that the exploded stuffing was speckled with mildew. The high, damp stink came from the couch. Strong enough to cut through the piss and shit smell, the stone smell, the river smell.

He got out his phone to take his own picture. He planned to text Mrs. Montessori and say something like *guess where I am*. But he saw a round, brown, slumbering object on the couch, on the cushions, right in the middle. It looked cleaner than everything else. He got closer and closer and saw that it was not, as he thought, a stray cat or raccoon.

A brown hat, with a high, round old-fashioned crown.

A bowler, a brown bowler. It had no mildew or mold on it, no water stains. As he stared at it, a slow movement in the corner of his eye made him leap back, almost fall. He turned to look. There was no one there. His hands shook, his legs felt rubbery, inflated. His heart was thudding and he was sweating. The hat was real. And warm, a lot warmer than he would have imagined given that it was sitting in the shade. The lining felt as warm as if it had just left a head. Montessori's hands still shook as he handled the hat (he told himself he had to, to make sure that it was real). He turned it once, twice in his hands. The last person he'd known to possess such a hat? Must have been his grandfather, or one of his great uncles. (Possibly even one of your uncles, as well.) It was clearly expensive, in addition to being clean.

A musical noise broke his consideration. He looked for the source and saw that the driver side window of his car was splintered in a round, irregular, striated pattern. He still had the hat in his hands as he raced back across the riverbank. He turned his ankle sharply and had to slow down and limp the rest of the way. The window was almost shattered, as if by a sure, single blow. Montessori saw the point of origin. There was no way it could have come from the road, and there was no one else nearby: he was alone on the bank, no other cars near the nature point. There seemed to be no other damage, and the weather was good. Montessori decided the safest thing would be to knock the rest of the glass out himself, rather than risk its breaking while he drove, and then have it repaired. The hat he placed on the hood of his car. He found a greasy rag in the tire kit in his trunk and wrapped it around his hand. He knocked the glass out from the inside, so that none would get on the seat. Before he drove off, he slipped the hat onto the passenger seat and stared through the broken window at the bridge. No one under it, no one at all.

He parked in the guarded lot on the office campus and locked the hat in his trunk before he went to his meetings. He wanted to make sure no one took it. That way he could bring it home. As evidence. Though he knew he could not say of what. The meetings went well, despite the pain in his foot and leg from turning his ankle. After he finished, his foot felt a bit better and even the thought of the broken car window failed to bother him. He had the hat and the hat had to mean something. He could drive directly to the garage and take the subway home; they could get along without the car for a few days while the window was fixed. As he was leaving the garage, the guard said:

I couldn't help noticing you left your window down the whole time the car was here. I would have contacted you but I know you're a guest so I don't have your office number.

Montessori said: It was broken on the way here. I don't really know how, while I was stopped.

The guard paused before he said: Did it look like someone had thrown a rock? A spiderweb pattern in the glass? But not fully broken?

Montessori was shocked. He nodded, his mouth dry.

The guard smiled and said: That's those kids. From the town. They climb up trees and shoot pellet guns. They're going to hurt someone someday. They break car windows and regular windows. It's a real hazard. That is the pattern. Everyone knows it by now. I imagine you never looked for a pellet.

Montessori had not, and he remembered he also had not checked the trees, not high up, not at all. The guard was still smiling. He had a large mole near his mouth that resembled a fly. Bristly, as if iridescent.

The evening was cool and smelled like grass and the cool air came in through the window while he drove to the garage. They told him there it would be a few days, but promised they'd have it fixed up good as new. Montessori almost left the hat in the car, on the passenger seat, but the garage guy had called out as he was leaving: don't forget your hat! He brought the hat home in a plastic bag they gave him. He wanted to decide when to show his wife, so he said nothing about the contents. She was sympathetic. She agreed with the parking lot guard that it must have been kids shooting pellet guns. Montessori had hidden the bag with the hat in it under their bed, to keep it out of sight. Once the kids were asleep – he heard their asynchronous snoring – he decided he was going to bring it out. While his wife was brushing her teeth, he got down to get the hat in the bag out from under the bed. His fingers touched the bag but it was empty. He pulled it out and sat with it between his knees as he stared stupidly into its depths.

His wife said, from the bathroom: What on earth are you doing?

Montessori said: One second.

He pushed himself under the bed – it was high enough off the ground for him to do this with ease – and pawed through the semidark. There were a few fluffy spheres of dust and some big-grained grit on the floor, as well as a quarter (quite cool to the touch). The hat was not there, not even when he pulled his whole body under and reached every single part of the under-bed zone, and not when he grabbed his phone from the night table and used the flashlight to check again.

When he emerged, Mrs. Montessori said: Seriously, what are you doing? Are you looking for something?

Montessori sat and said nothing for a while. Without the hat, what was the point? But his wife squatted down next to him and put her hand on the back of his neck. She was smiling, stroking his neck gently. His younger son's high snores rose and fell.

Montessori said: I found a hat.

His wife said: What?

Montessori said: I passed the bridge. You know, in the photo with the dead couch – the one the cop showed us? I passed that bridge on my way up to the meeting and I stopped and checked under it. To see if the couch was still there. I don't know why. And on the couch I found a hat. I brought it back here in this bag, and now it's gone.

His wife said: Why did you steal a hat?

Montessori said: I don't really know.

And he didn't, to be honest. Because while it had vaguely resembled in shape the hat in the drawing, it had nothing else to do with their current situation. His wife was still smiling. Her eyes kind and slightly narrowed.

His wife said: One of the kids must have gotten it. We can check in the morning.

Montessori said: It sounds crazy, but I really did find a hat. Like an old-fashioned hat. And I just needed to bring it back. Right?

His wife shrugged and said: One of the boys obviously has it. No one can resist a hat. You proved that yourself.

Montessori had a lot of trouble that night. Every time he heard a sound, even a minor one, it woke him up. He kept thinking about the hat. How stupid it was he had brought it home. How stupid it was that now it had vanished. She must be right. One of the boys must have taken it. In the morning, Montessori asked them both at breakfast. Josep had not seen such a hat, and neither had his younger son.

Montessori said: Are you sure? No one's in trouble, I brought it home and I just want to make sure it didn't vanish into thin air.

His younger son stared down at the table, looking into his cereal.

He said: Are you absolutely, positively sure?

His younger son took a large bite of cereal and then started to cough. Milk and chewed cereal sprayed from his mouth on the table. Mrs. Montessori was patting their younger son on the back. Josep got up to go and finish getting ready, shaking his head and snorting contemptuously. Their younger son needed a fresh shirt, but still stoically shook his head when asked – Montessori pushed his luck – a few more times about the hat. Montessori found that he was having more and more trouble biting back his laughs. After the boys left the house and Mrs. Montessori left for her office, he burst into a deep, tussic gale. It doubled him over, left him breathless and red faced.

Montessori planned to work remotely while he would be without his car. There was no need for him to be in the office and the subway ride was a long one, complicated by the fact that they were doing repairs on the line he used. First thing after he had sent the few emails he needed to, he checked his younger son's room for the hat. It had to be there. He looked in the closet, under the bed, in the desk drawers. Old Abel helped him, leaping from bed to desk to dresser. Montessori found no hat. His younger son had not hidden it in the hall closet or either of the bathroom linen closets. What was left? Josep's room. No hat there, either. The cat looped between Montessori's ankles as he searched. Had the boy taken it to the attic? He was scared to go up there alone or with his brother. On the other hand, Montessori had to know. It was hotter up there, the air a little stuffy and stale. No hat there, either. It was not in the kitchen or dining room, not in the coat closet, not in the basement or out on the patio. The last place Montessori looked was the living room. He hesitated before squatting down to look under the sofa, the new one. He had to lift up the blankets to peer. Old Abel screeched and shot away.

More laughter. From where? Montessori, it seemed. The hat was there. He pulled it out. It was covered in a thick, undisturbed film of dust as if it had been there for days or weeks.

He carried the hat to the dining table and photographed it and texted the picture to his wife. He hung it afterwards on a wooden peg stuck in the wall near the downstairs bathroom. There he could keep an eye on it while he worked. He left the gray dust film on it, except where his fingers had smeared it away. The dust film glowed a little in the sunlight. It really did look like the hat in the drawing. It had the same shape, the same stubby brim. Even the flattened perspective of the drawing could not conceal that. That did not mean anything by itself. Hats tended to assume certain shapes. As for the dust: That might have happened because it was simply very dusty under the sofa and the hat happened to pick some up. Enough to make a film like that. His son could have disturbed the dust when he hid the hat. It could have settled on the crown and brim again. His phone made the text sound and he felt lightly triumphant. What would his wife say now? The message failed to send, so he tried again.

The afternoon was warm and breezy, so he ate lunch at a place near his house with outside tables. He brought his computer with him, in case of emergencies, and he ended up staying there until almost five working. The boys both had soccer practice that afternoon and would not be home until seven. The texts he tried to send to his wife refused to go through, even though he restarted his phone a few times, and when he tried to email himself the photo, it was too large to attach (though he checked the file size and it was below the limit). He did not feel like dealing with it, so he gave up. When he got back home, the boys were there.

Josep said: Practice ended early. Coach Musil had a training course.

They were both wearing the all-black uniforms of the team, and they were both covered in tawny dust from the field. They gulped down water.

Then Montessori saw that the hat was gone from the wall peg.

He said: Did one of you take the hat?

His younger son said: What hat, dad?

He would not meet Montessori's eyes. Montessori got down on his knees, face to face with him and took him by the shoulders. He felt a sudden, blazing tension in his arms, his hands, his jaw.

He said: Did you take the hat? Tell me, did you take the hat?

His younger son looked down. He wiped at his face with his thin, warm arm.

Montessori said: I am going to ask you one more time. Did you take the hat? Did you put it somewhere?

His younger son said: No, no, I promise.

The boy's voice was shaking. Josep stepped closer.

He said: Dad, it's OK, it's just a hat.

Montessori rose up. His movement pushed his younger son aside hard enough that the boy caromed into the table and stood there, eyes wide, mouth wide, a tear slipping down and cutting a clean trace through the golden dust on his face.

Montessori said: It's not OK. It is not, and I am beyond tired of you and your fucking bullshit!

His voice had risen to a naked shout by the time he finished. He was breathing hard. He felt a little sick, a little dizzy, and flushed with uncertain pleasure. Josep moved to stand in front of his brother. Josep was taller than ever, it seemed. The hat would have been right at eye level for him.

Josep said: Dad, calm down. Seriously.

A swift, gray movement behind the boys distracted him. Like the flicker of a curtain. It ended before Montessori had a chance to look at it full on. His breathing was loud and damp. The hitching breaths of his younger son came through it. The boy was whimpering a little.

Montessori picked up his younger son. As he lifted him up, the boy said: Daddy! Daddy!

Montessori was swaying. Josep looked at him, his face blank and stiff.

His younger son said: I'm sorry! Daddy! I'm sorry!

That night, Montessori sat in the backyard after dinner. He wanted a drink but he refused himself one. He had seltzer. Old Abel watched, pressed against the kitchen window, as the boys kicked a soccer ball back and forth. His younger son was still a little dirty but smiling and happy. Montessori caught Josep giving him wary glances once in a while, but that was all. Mrs. Montessori joined them – she had come back from her run. The boys went on playing for a while and then went inside to finish their homework.

Once they were inside, Montessori shut the back door and said: I want to get rid of the sofa. I am calling the haulers tonight. There's a 24-hour service I found.

Mrs. Montessori took a long sip from her wine. The wine was red and the golden light from the external lamps flickered in it.

She said: Why all of a sudden?

Montessori felt too embarrassed to go on about the hat, about his outburst. The hat was gone now, anyway. She had never seen it. Not the hat itself, not the image of it. Wait! A sudden idea came to him.

He said: Look.

He got out his phone and scrolled through the photos until he found the one from that morning. The one he had tried to send her, that had failed to go through. Now when he looked, he saw only a blank, black square. No image at all.

Mrs. Montessori said: What's that?

Montessori found he was furious again. This time he let out a long breath and stayed silent until he was calmer. His wife took another long sip of her wine.

Montessori said: I tried to take a picture of the hat.

Mrs. Montessori said: What hat?

Montessori said: The hat I found on the couch under the bridge. Now it's gone again. Remember? I found it under the sofa this morning. The new sofa. Then I took a picture of it and hung it up. And now it's gone. I don't think the boys did it.

Mrs. Montessori said: Yes, I heard about that.

Her face was hard. She drank more wine.

Montessori said: I just want the sofa out of here.

Mrs. Montessori said: I think it's extremely fucked up that you are trying to blame a sofa for your behavior.

She said nothing more. Neither did Montessori. She finished her wine and went inside. Montessori stayed outside. He tried four times to call the 24-hour haulers. The first three no one answered. He finally got someone on the fourth. It turned out that they no longer operated on a 24-hour schedule, despite their advertising, but that they could come either tomorrow or Friday.

Montessori said: Tomorrow, please.

The operator said: And how big is the load?

Montessori said: It's just one sofa, about five feet wide and two feet deep, maybe three feet high.

The operator fell silent now. Montessori waited.

The operator said: We don't usually take jobs that small on an expedited basis. But I will send someone over tomorrow, OK? You still have to pay the minimum carriage fee, though. I can email you the fee schedule.

Montessori took all the blankets off the sofa and put them back in the blanket closet. His sons were asleep and so was his wife: he heard their asynchronous snores. The sound filled him with peace, as it always did (even when he and his wife had been fighting). He sat in the armchair, drinking more seltzer, and staring at the now denuded sofa. Was the stale, damp smell coming back? He sniffed, got closer, sniffed again. Hard to say. He even stuck his head fully under the sofa to have a good look around.

Then the first-floor bathroom toilet flushed and he heard the sink faucet turn on. He struck his head, hard, on the sofa frame leaping back from under it and rushing to the door. He opened it. The water was running. Plainly running. The toilet finished its musical rustle. Montessori stared at the sink faucet handle, pushed all the way to the left for maximum hot water, and at the steam starting to rise up from the water as it streamed into the drain. Was this supposed to scare him? Fuck that. He shut off the faucet. The handle was cold, cold enough that it burned his fingers a little as he touched it. The cold burning lingered as he rubbed the fingers on his shirt. There was a silvery veil of condensing moisture on the faucet handle. It was already covering up the marks his fingers had left in it.

Fuck the haulers. He was doing it himself. The sofa, when he lifted it, was not as heavy as he'd thought. He got it to the back door without any difficulty and almost all the way across the yard. Then he felt a cold, fiery twinge in his right foot – the same one he had turned while walking back from the bridge with the hat in his hand – and fell to one knee. The sofa, awkward and wide, tumbled him the rest of the way down. A similar pain flamed through his lower back. He stood up and leaned against the fence. His leg throbbed and so did his back. He was not going to give up now. He opened the rear gate and propped it with a fragment of brick he found in the alley. He took hold of the sofa and dragged it across the last flagstones of the gate path and out into the alley, next to the trashcans. Even this lesser effort worsened his foot and back pain, and when he was done he sat with his legs out and his back propped against the alley side of the fence. He did not know whether he would be able to get back to the house under his own power.

Soon, however, his foot felt better. He was able to limp back into the kitchen and up the stairs. He took a handful of aspirin and climbed into the bed next to his wife, who did not interrupt her snoring. He had his phone with him in case the haulers called back. He suspected they would not. This mattered less now that the sofa was out of the house. By the time he fell asleep his phone still had not rung.

The pain in his foot was almost gone by the morning, but the pain in his back was worse. It woke him up well before dawn and he was unable to get back to sleep. The day was hot and the air already damp. His wife was sleeping, silently now, almost immobile under the sheet. He went downstairs to make coffee, holding the banister the whole trip and staggering. He had to rest on the lowest step to give the back pain time to recede. He felt weak and dizzy. He had never injured his back before, though he had long dreaded doing so. Before the pain had fully receded, he saw that the sofa was back in the living room, more or less right where it had been.

His cry was loud and involuntary. He bit it back as soon as he himself heard it. He stayed on the steps, panting a little and staring into the living room. He heard his wife get up, heard the upstairs toilet flush, heard her pad down the hall and onto the steps. Her ankles brushed him as she moved past him and on into the kitchen. By the time he had gathered enough strength to join her, she had already made her coffee and was staring into a magazine. She did not look up or speak to him as he fixed his own coffee, not even when he sat directly across from her at the kitchen table. Montessori did not want to speak first, even about the sofa. He drank in silence as his wife looked back and forth in the magazine. He was getting a little restless when she shifted her face up.

She said: It's even more fucked up what you did with the sofa. I never thought you would have done something like that.

Montessori said: What do you mean.

She said: I woke up last night. I saw the sofa out by the trash. So I brought it back in. I never thought you'd have done something like that. You need to deal with your own problems, not blame them on some fucking sofa!

He put his hand on her forearm and she did not jerk it away. He still had to say something, he couldn't just go on sitting there.

He said: I'll try, I promise.

His wife looked up at him and said: Your anger is toxic and poisonous, you know that, right?

Montessori said: I do, I know.

They held hands until the boys came down and Montessori made them breakfast. His foot was completely healed but his back was hurting more and more. It seemed odd that his wife had been able to get the sofa in without hurting her back, but she was more flexible than he was. He did not mention the sofa again. He knew it would only make her angry. He found that his vision kept returning to it, however, and when she took their younger son to school and Josep had left on his own, he was glad to be able to have another uninterrupted look at it. The legs were scuffed from dragging, and a feather of grass was stuck to the back. It was damp again; the stale damp smell had returned (not as strong as before). The simplest thing would be to break it apart. Right now. He had a hammer, saws. It was an old sofa and he knew that wrecking it could not be difficult. But his back hurt too much for him to walk fast, let alone attack a sofa with tools.

He could also have the haulers come for it, to pay any price and have them come for it now. He called them once more. He again found that he could not get through. At last someone answered, and Montessori explained the situation. That he had called last night, that he still needed a sofa taken away. That he had injured his back. That he would pay all expedited-service fees.

The man on the phone said: Is this Mr. Montessori? You called last night?

Montessori said: Yes, yes.

The man on the phone said: We don't appreciate people wasting our time. We sent a truck over to your place late last night. No sofa by the curb. What were you thinking?

Montessori said: It was in the alley!

The man on the phone said: We can't go in alleys because of insurance reasons, and we don't appreciate people wasting our time. Please consult another service for your transportation needs.

Then he hung up. Montessori hurled his cellphone at the sofa. It struck the cushions with a limp thump. His back pain flared again as he threw, so much that he had to sit down again and pant until it started to ease. His phone was ringing too, now, but his back hurt so much he failed to reach the phone before it had stopped. He saw that it was the hauling company. He tried them back. They did not answer.

What could he do?

Another hauler. He tried every one he could find on the internet. There were eleven. Three had closed down; two failed to answer; the remaining five could not schedule anything before the week after next. This was the busy season for haulers, the summer prompted people to throw away their belongings. He settled on the date the last company he called offered, more than two weeks away. He offered the woman on the phone a thousand dollars – he called it a convenience fee – if they could come sooner. This week. Tomorrow. She tittered emptily, like he had made an ugly joke. He settled on the far-off date and he was glad he did. When he doubled back and spoke to the others, they no longer had openings in that range. Now it was a month. They also failed to respond to the offered money, in three cases hanging up as soon as he mentioned it. He sent emails to the two companies that had not answered their phones, just in case something was open, and in the email he made the same "convenience fee" offer.

That still left too much time. At least it was something. His back hurt less now so he limped over to the armchair and sat and stared at the sofa. The smell was back, strong and humid. Though the windows were open and the ceiling fan was on.

Setting it on fire was too risky. The fire could spread and burn the rest of the house. If he could get it back out into the yard at some point that might work, however. Even if it meant he'd end up having to pay a ticket: You were not allowed to burn trash in your yard in the city. If his back got better, he could also disassemble it. That seemed like the safest and simplest approach to use, but it required his back pain to stop. There was also the NEVER SPEND MONEY website. This his wife used sometimes to give away things that the family no longer needed (and once to obtain a set of bronze quail-shaped paperweights). People would take almost anything, as long as it was free. That method meant depending on others for help. His wife had mentioned that sometimes she saw things stay up without being taken for months at a time.

Whatever he did, he had to do while he was at home and his wife was at work. She thought he was trying to blame the sofa for his outburst at the boys, for their younger son's stricken face, and any disposal effort she would insist was more of the same. No, it had to be a fait accompli. He'd have to take his chances. In the meantime? He thought while he stroked Old Abel. The cat was stiff, clearly a little frightened. Montessori decided that until his back had improved – he hoped by tomorrow or the day after – there was not that much he could do other than keep calm. The cat purred and butted his warm head into Montessori's open palm, making soft chirps the whole time.

After waiting a while to make sure that the first-floor toilet was not flushing and that the faucet was not turning on, Montessori decided to spend the morning working at the cafe. He did not like sitting in the house, smelling the damp smell. His back pain was starting to recede. As long as he did not make any harsh, sudden movements, he should be OK. He felt better as soon as he sat down. It was a warm, sunlit, greenish day. There were just enough people in the cafe to provide a soothing hum of conversation without it being obtrusive (as it would have been with many more or many fewer customers). To his own surprise, despite the pain in his back and his exhaustion, he felt hungry. He ordered a large breakfast, something he almost never did, and began to hammer away at the valuation prepared by his junior assessors. They had done a good, clean job. This also surprised Montessori. His younger colleagues were usually lazy and slipshod. The work absorbed Montessori until almost noon. He took breaks only to walk slowly up to the counter and order more coffee. After his fifth cup (he had not realized it was so many) he felt the need to urinate.

A mirror hung on the lilac wall above the toilet tank. Right where a tallish man (as Montessori was) could look into his own eyes while pissing. Urinating sent a pleasurable pain through his back. He shut his eyes to savor it. He opened them again and saw he was not alone.

In the mirror, right behind him, stood a shorter gentleman wearing a brown bowler hat. He stood there long enough for Montessori to see his spectacles and mustache.

Montessori struck out at the mirror before he could stop himself. He shattered it with the soft edge of his fist and felt the blood run at once. His back also started to hurt much more badly (though not as badly as after he had thrown the phone). The mirror was cracked in a rough, ellipsoid pattern. Like the concentric rings of a spider's web. It swayed a little on the wall and the glass sang. Montessori was worried it would fall out but it did not. He knew he needed first to stop the bleeding and then to hide the damage. That way he could get out of the cafe with no problems. He wrapped his hand in paper towels and lifted the garbage can up (fortunately it was light, cheap plastic) right under the mirror and dumped the whole thing in. The glass collapsed outwards as he moved. While it was falling, Montessori thought he glimpsed again that brown hat, those wet eyes and lenses. He looked away before he could confirm it.

Back in the cafe, he kept his bloodied hand in his pocket as he stuffed his computer and pen and paper into his laptop bag with his left hand. The girl behind the counter – was she a classmate of Josep's? He knew her from somewhere – stared the whole time. His hand was still bleeding but not as badly by the time he got home. He cleaned the cut with peroxide, squeezed in antibiotic ointment and covered it with gauze and a bandage. It was too big to use band-aids. His wife would be home soon and he needed to come up with an excuse. Otherwise she would realize at once that it was part of the sofa affair, and her recriminations would begin all over again. He decided to tell her that he had cut himself while slicing steak for a sandwich. That would have to suffice.

Then he walked through every room in the house that had a mirror and stared into each one in turn. Staring until his eyes dried out and throbbed, until he was forced to blink. He did not see the figure again. No hat, no spectacles, no mustache. His back hurt as he came near the end of the task. As he examined the last mirror, the one hung up on the narrow wall between the attic dormers, he heard through the deep silence of the house the first-floor bathroom toilet flush and the faucet turn on. He hobbled down as quickly as he could – the pain was almost as bad as the first pain now – and opened the door.

The faucet was running. The handle frigid and veiled with frost. He shut off the water as the toilet gave out its musical rustle.

Montessori made sure to keep calm the rest of the afternoon and evening. His wife was in a better mood and the boys seemed to have forgotten his anger entirely. His wife was even solicitous about the wound on his hand, and his younger son eagerly offered to help cut up Montessori's food for dinner and then to bring Montessori a beer, which the boy insisted on opening himself. He avoided looking at the sofa as well. His wife, though she was smiling and happy, was nonetheless watching him, and he could not make any mistakes. Yes, he was angry about having to conceal the truth. He was angrier about the injustice being done to him. It was the sofa's fault, not his! Still, from an outside perspective, it looked like he was guilty. After all, he was the one who had to run out of the cafe that afternoon, like a thief.

He had a bad moment while he was going to bed. He thought he saw the hat, spectacles and mustache in the large mirror hung above the bedroom dresser. They were not there, or they had gone too quickly to be sure of, and his wife was not present to see the grimace his face assumed. He even developed another strategy too, right as she was coming in. If she did catch him making any grimaces, he could blame his back pain. Which was not getting much better, although it also wasn't getting much worse.

The moon was almost full that night and the sky was clear, blue-black. The moonlight came through the window and appeared in the dresser mirror. The reflected, subtle glow filtered in. Though he admired moonlight, old silver. Now it felt (he realized) as though a cool, clerical gaze was resting upon him.

He maintained his calm through the next morning, despite his exhaustion and back pain. His day was almost empty, luckily, other than the notes he needed to give the junior assessors on their valuation document. At first he thought he would go to the cafe. Then he remembered. He could never go back there, unless he wanted the police to get involved (more than they already had been). He did not want to stay in the house. The impulse to check the mirrors all the time was too strong, and the smell from the sofa also persisted (though maybe a little fainter?). So he decided to take care of some chores. They needed lightbulbs and toilet paper. Easy enough to obtain. There was a bag full of dry cleaning he needed to drop off, and some that had been left at the cleaners for more than two weeks.

Old Abel wound himself around Montessori's legs as he was getting ready to leave. The cat was strong, despite his age, and he almost succeeded in tripping Montessori. Montessori picked him up and tried to soothe him, to stroke him. The cat yowled and chirped, waving his narrow, handsome head. The sunlight flashed on his green eyes. Montessori set him down and dashed out. The cat followed but Montessori got the door shut before he could escape. The cat remained in the front window, chirping and yowling, as Montessori headed to the drug store.

There were mirrors overhead there. He knew they were meant to help employees see if anyone was stealing. The store was empty except for Montessori and the clerk. Montessori glanced upwards all the same as he shopped. No mustache, bowler or spectacles appeared.

The man who owned the dry cleaners recognized him right away.

He said: Mr. Montessori! It's been a while!

He turned on the u-shaped carousel that brought clothes to and from the rear of the shop. It hummed and soon Montessori's clothes appeared. The black suit he had worn to a friend's funeral, his wife's black and white silk dress, three neckties and a trench coat. As he was paying, Montessori noticed a paper tag affixed to the outer plastic sleeve: J. MEERVERMESSER & ASSOC., DRY CLEANING PRODUCTS.

The name made his mouth go dry. That was the one solid result he had gotten during his internet search, when the sofa first arrived.

He said: Is this where you get your supplies?

He pointed at the label. The shop owner nodded.

Montessori said: It's not out of business?

The shop owner said: No, I just got a shipment from them the other day. Why do you ask? Are you also in dry cleaning?

Montessori shook his head and left. The tag gave a phone number, an email, and an address. It was not far away. It was even in Queens. No one answered when he called. He had expected that. He stood with his phone pressed to his ear, the plastic sleeve flapping in a soft breeze. He stopped at his house and tossed the dry cleaning onto the dining room table. He checked his email: nothing major. The boys had soccer practice and would be home late. The damp smell was still there, mild and strong. He changed the bandage on his wounded hand – the flesh around the cut was a little inflated, he saw, and he squeezed in more antibiotic ointment – and swallowed a few aspirin. He walked to the subway and went down the stairs to the gate. He got to the platform just as a train was arriving. He boarded it and found himself alone in the car. The vibrations made his back hurt a little worse, so he slumped and tried to relax. It was going to be a longish ride. He wished he had brought a book with him. He thought about J. MEERVERMESSER & ASSOC. They must have come back into business. They had changed boroughs. The first address he saw, the dead one, had been in the Bronx. In Kingsbridge. It was stupid to go and see them, he suspected. And was that a mustache? Was that a hat, in the smeary window? When he looked, really looked, however, there was nothing. Only the tunnel darkness.

The building J. MEERVERMESSER & ASSOC. had their new offices in was short and brownish. It looked like all the other buildings near the train station, and people were going in and out of the lobby as they would the lobby of any other building. The offices were on the fourth floor. Montessori went right in, feeling less and less sure of himself as the elevator ascended. The suite belonging to the company was at the end of the long, silent central corridor. A dentist-office light filled the corridor. A silent thick hum. Montessori's back and hand hurt (but not his foot) as he pressed the plastic doorbell. Chimes sounded inside. A buzzer. He opened the door and walked through.

The office was similar to the corridor. White walls, hard dental light. The carpet gray and a little dusty. The reception area was small and square, with windows overlooking the train tracks. There were taupe couches and a small desk. TVs on the walls with a show about bauxite mining on them. At the desk sat a man in a blue uniform. He smiled at Montessori as he walked in. He had a large mole near his mouth that resembled a fly. Bristly, as if iridescent.

He said: Can I help you, sir?

The desk man looked a little familiar, Montessori noted. He took a big breath and swallowed some saliva; he had to go on.

He said: I know it's stupid, but I recently came into possession of an object associated with the name of your company. And this is the only person or business I can find with that name. I never heard the name before.

The desk man said: Yes, it's certainly unusual.

Montessori said: I was wondering if you had any information about the name. Where it comes from. This object is old. I thought there might be some connection.

The desk man said: What is it?

Montessori said: It's a sofa.

The desk man said: I know very little about the name. But it does come from our founder. Back in the nineteenth century. Would you like to see him? We have a painting up.

At this, Montessori felt better. The desk man was already getting up. Montessori knew him from somewhere. Knew the voice, knew the mole near the mouth, with bristles. He led Montessori down one of the short passages that extended from the waiting area. They passed open and closed office doors. Through the open doors he saw men and women sitting at desks, typing away, muttering into phones. One woman in a violet dress was unrolling a wide chart covered with hexagonal diagrams of chemical compounds. She looked right at Montessori with an insulted frown when she caught him staring. At the end of the corridor was a small, sunny room. The air was still and it glittered with dust. There was an empty desk and a wooden chair, nothing much. Like what you might find in a teacher's lounge. On the wall was a framed oil portrait.

Montessori stared. At first, the resemblance was powerful. The man wore a bowler, brown, and had spectacles, black. A bowler and spectacles he had seen before. As he came closer – the smiling desk man stood to one side with his arm out, like an usher – Montessori saw the resemblance fading. This man seemed older. He had fluffy white hair and in addition to the mustache a goatee. The shape of the face was different. Less round, more vulpine.

The smiling desk man said: Frankly, I don't know too much more. But this is the portrait of our founder. We moved it here from our old offices.

Montessori was close enough now to see the slimy, blinding highlights on the thicker peaks of the brushwork. Up close, there were some points of connection. That could not be denied, though the resemblance was not definitive.

The smiling desk man said: Is there anything else?

Montessori said: Would you be interested in a furniture donation? For this room, I mean.

The desk man, walking back toward the exit, said: No, no, we can't accept donations. Because we work with chemicals. The law prohibits it.

They passed the offices again, and the violet-dress woman was gone. Montessori saw the compound-diagram chart taped up over a window, sunlight pouring through it. Faint shadows made an irregular, spiderweb pattern on the paper. In the front room the smiling desk man – to Montessori's surprise – shook his hand.

Montessori said: This is strange to say, but have we met before?

The desk man said: Yes. The wages for parking-lot security guards are not much. So I have to work two jobs to get by. Did you ever get your car window fixed?

Montessori said: I am working on it.

Out on the street he tried to see the window with the chemical chart taped over it. The angle was bad, all he saw was the white glare from the sun. Was it him, was it the shitheaded, silent, and sneaky motherfucker in the picture, or no? Montessori failed to decide. Too late, on the train, he thought of having offered to buy the portrait. The company might not have sold it. The smiling desk man needed money. He and Montessori could have worked something out; he'd have had leisure (assuming they made a deal) to examine the face, the mustache, the bowler. Even draw spectacles on it, to make sure. Right before his stop, the train halted in the tunnel. It was hot in the car. The air conditioning was not on. Montessori was alone. There was no announcement explaining why the train had stopped. For a moment, the lights even flickered. In the sudden, brief darkness, Montessori felt rising panic. The light came back on and the train started moving again.

It was much hotter when he came out of the train. He was sweating by the time he reached his own street. He saw from the corner that police cars had gathered and he panicked once more. He raced up, despite the pain in his hand and back. They were not gathered in front of his house, he saw, but in front of old

Señor Periander's. There was an ambulance, its back bay door open wide. The front door of Señor Periander's house hung open too. Two cops were standing around out front, and a tubby medic sat on the rear bay lip of the ambulance. They all looked up when Montessori arrived, as if they had been waiting for him. His back ached worse and worse and his hand, under the bandage, throbbed. It felt tender and swollen.

He said: What happened?

The tubby medic said: It's nothing to worry about sir, we got a call.

The cops looked at Montessori. Neither spoke. Montessori heard a rattling. It got louder and louder. Almost like a musical rustle. Another medic was walking backwards through the front door, guiding a metal gurney. The gurney produced the musical rustle as one loose side-rail clattered. Another medic was guiding the foot of the gurney. Strapped to it, Montessori saw, was Señor Periander. As the medics steered him past, Montessori glimpsed the grayish face, slack mouth. An oxygen mask was clamped over it, and the chest under the white sheet rose and fell a little. The eyes were slack too. At least until they slid over Montessori. Then they went wide, active, and the old man tried to lift up a hand. The eyes (watery gray) stayed on Montessori as the medics moved the gurney over the curb, staring and staring. Señor Periander fell back, slack again, as the medics hefted the gurney up onto the lip of the rear bay.

The silence in his own house pressed down on Montessori when he walked in. His hand throbbed harder and harder and his back was hurting him so much he needed to lie down. From his bedroom window he could see into Señor Periander's yard: the deck chair he sat in usually was turned over, a newspaper lay fluttering, spread out over the grass, and the black, round eye of the coffee cup looked right back at Montessori. As he was lying there, he heard the downstairs toilet flush and the faucet turn on, but he covered his head with the pillow.

That's how the boys found him. The noise of their coming home had failed to wake him. The slightly sticky, warm and dusty hand of his younger son on his forehead woke him up.

He said: Daddy, are you OK? You look sick?

Montessori sat up. He smiled at his younger son and palmed the top of his head. The boy smiled back, eyes wide and bright. The toilet sound from downstairs had stopped and the faucet sound, too.

Josep said: How's your hand, dad?

Montessori said: It's getting better, I think.

He explained what had happened to Señor Periander over dinner. Mrs. Montessori found it very upsetting. Josep and his brother listened eagerly. Montessori was careful how he spoke. He knew he could not let his wife see what he actually suspected. He refused to even glance into the living room, so he would not give himself away.

That night, as they were lying in bed, his wife asked: Did they mention what hospital?

Montessori said: No, they wouldn't say.

Mrs. Montessori said: Oh, that's so awful. Does he have any relatives?

Montessori said: I don't know. I never saw any kids there, did you?

Mrs. Montessori said: We should find out. Bring him flowers or something.

Montessori said: yes, I agree.

The next morning his hand felt much better. He took off the bandage and saw that the wound was already beginning to close up, that the inflammation around the edges was dying down. It hardly hurt at all, in fact, even when he touched it. He put on more antibiotic ointment and a fresh bandage, and the pain vanished almost entirely. His back pain was much better as well, though he still felt a twinge if he tried to move too quickly. His car was supposed to be ready that morning. His good luck with his injuries made him suspicious. He called the garage as soon as it opened, and they told him everything was good. Montessori felt relieved.

After his wife had gone to work and the boys left, he drank his coffee in the kitchen. No noise from the bathroom, none at all. He saw that the overturned deck chair, the newspaper and coffee cup were still sitting out in Señor Periander's yard. His back was hurting a bit less, so he let himself in through the alley gate and righted the deck chair. The dew had disintegrated the newspaper. He gathered the shreds and threw them out. He picked up the coffee cup. He was going to take it inside, check around, lock the doors. He found that he could go no farther than the threshold of the back door. Calm, grayish light filled the inside. He ended up taking the cup back home with him, washing it and putting it in his own cabinet. He'd give it to Señor Periander when he returned from the hospital.

He left for the garage. It was just opening when he arrived. The mechanic unlocking the place and turning on the lights squinted at him when he gave his name and showed the parts manifest and bill they had emailed him. Montessori felt dizzy, once more: had they taken his car? The squint loosened and the mechanic was smiling.

He said: Oh, Miklos took this in. Sorry, I was not working that day. Should be right over here.

The car was clean and shining. A fresh coat of. The broken window replaced by a clean new pane. The mechanic opened the garage doors and told Montessori to turn it on to test it out. The window rolled up and down perfectly, smoothly. Montessori saw that the interior had been cleaned and detailed as well. All the dust and crumbs gone, everything wiped down, the seats scrubbed-looking. A green, pine-tree shaped air freshener hung from the stalk of the rearview mirror.

Montessori said: There's no cleaning fee in the bill, how much do I owe for that?

The mechanic said: No charge, that's a complimentary service we provide.

He took Montessori into his office to run his credit card. Again, Montessori expected disaster for a moment. The card went through. Montessori included a large tip. The mechanic thanked him and walked off into the huge parts racks in the back of the shop and Montessori returned to his car. He cried out again and was grateful the sudden whine of a high-pressure air hose blanked it out. There, on the passenger seat, was the bowler hat. Also clean, the dust brushed away. Visible tracks in the crown's nap.

Throw it away, crush it beneath his shoe, tear it apart: Montessori considered all these. He forced himself to shut the passenger door and got in on the driver's side. He had to hurry, he still needed to shower and change before going into the office. The hat stayed where it was while the car was parked in his driveway, and it stayed where it was while he drove into the city. Sunlight made it glow and then shadows stroked it. Sitting on the passenger seat as if it were his own. Still clean, still dustless. For a moment he thought he saw a mustache and spectacles in the rearview mirror. No, he had seen nothing.

At the office, he greeted the junior assessors as usual. He found in his email the revised valuation report he had requested. He occupied himself with that for most of the morning. The writer had done, to his surprise, an excellent job taking his revisions, and the document was more or less clean. He could begin setting up the transaction itself as soon as next week. True, his calm was dented by the fact that he feared seeing the mustache, spectacles, and bowler. There were no mirrors in his office, but there was plenty of mildly reflective glass. Every smear of shadow brought Montessori to attention. The men's room was especially difficult. A huge mirror backed the long stone counter, behind the sinks. It reflected the whole width of the room. The stalls were all empty, which made Montessori's anticipation worse. Nothing appeared.

That afternoon, Montessori called the junior assessors and the transaction specialist into the conference room. They occupied almost the whole table, only the two seats at the foot were empty. Montessori explained how pleased he was with the work they had all done, and that they were now ready to move the project into its next phase. He was getting ready to finish his thought, to say that he knew they would all work just as hard on the transaction phase of the project. As he started to speak he saw, sitting in one of the two empty chairs at the table foot, a plumpish, roundish figure. Glasses, spectacles, bowler. He was spinning the bowler from hand to hand and smiling emptily. Not at Montessori, but near him. The bowler hissed slightly as it passed over the table. Montessori heard it but his colleagues even at that end of the table seemed to notice nothing. His hand was throbbing, harder and harder. It felt like the blood was rushing and pumping under the skin.

Everyone was looking at him. At him, at him! Not the motherfucker with the spectacles, the mustache, the spinning hat. The injustice was worse than the pain, than his dry, cavernous mouth. Montessori swallowed a few times and came up with a dry cough.

Then he said: And I wanted to thank you all very much. We can talk more later.

There was another silence as Montessori's colleagues realized the meeting was over. Their normal smiles returned and walked out (in the shuffling way people adopt in large offices). Montessori stayed there, staring at the pencil and pad he had brought in. When he forced himself to look up, the spinning hat and all other eventuations were gone. Montessori did not see anything, not even a glimpse, for the rest of the day. His hand hurt. Not as badly as it had before. The hat was still on the passenger seat when he got his car from the building garage. It shone a little, silently, as he drove home. The lights were on in his house, he saw as he arrived. Mrs. Montessori and the boys were sitting at the dinner table. Josep was talking and his mother and younger brother were smiling. Mrs. Montessori held a glass of dark wine. Montessori sat in his car for a long time before he went inside. He forced a smile onto his face and ignored the pain in his hand.

Josep said: Hey dad, I got a job!

He had been hired by the cafe where Montessori had seen the bowler, spectacles, and mustache in the mirror. It was under new management and they were increasing their workforce. Josep's friend already worked there. Montessori listened and smiled even harder. He had been right. The girl who served him his coffee was Josep's friend.

His younger son said: I got a job too, I am studying rabies!

About Montessori's hand, Mrs. Montessori was solicitous. She helped change his bandage – the cut at least did not *look* as bad; the swelling had abated totally, there was no pus, and the lips were almost closed. The pain was worse. She added more antibiotic ointment and even got him an ice pack after the new bandage was on. The cold soothed it. Montessori took ibuprofen as well, and that helped too.

Once he was settled, Mrs. Montessori said: I can't believe he got a job! I am so proud of him, and he is getting so old.

Montessori said: He'll be in college in less than two years.

Mrs. Montessori said: Oh my god.

He was unable to sleep at all that night. The pain in his hand kept him awake. At moments it felt hot and swollen, at other times almost numb, but it never stopped aching and throbbing. The ice pack did not help, more ibuprofen did nothing. He felt grateful the next day was a Saturday, that he had no business responsibilities to deal with. The cold, clerical gaze of the mirror. That was a problem too. He tried covering it up with a blanket but that did nothing, and he took the blanket off after a while because he did not want his wife to see it.

Saturday was also Josep's first day of work. His younger brother made him a card that said HAPPY WORK DAY. Josep went off early. He was on the first shift. As a junior employee he had to work the first shift for a while. After he was gone, his younger brother started making him another card.

Mrs. Montessori said: We should go there for lunch.

Montessori said: No, it would only embarrass him.

Mrs. Montessori said: Don't be such a skeptic. He might pretend to be embarrassed but he'll be happy, and we can leave him a big tip.

Their younger son said: Yeah, and I can give him his second card.

Montessori saw how it was impossible for him to refuse. His wife was looking at him, her smile hardening, her gaze going rigid. His hand hurt worse and worse. He smiled, as he had done the previous night.

He said: You know what? That's a great idea.

Their younger son worked on the card for the rest of the morning. Montessori counted on his phone calendar. It was eleven days until the haulers could come. His hand was throbbing. Upstairs, his wife sang loudly and randomly in the shower. He sat in the kitchen, drinking coffee to wake himself up. Though he suspected it was coming, when he heard the toilet in the downstairs bathroom flush and the faucet turn on, he still felt a violent, physical shock.

He said to his younger son: Did you hear that?

The boy drew his tiny, pink tongue back into his mouth. He had extruded it in concentration.

He said: Hear what, daddy?

He smiled up at Montessori. There was a green-black ink smear on the tip of his nose.

Montessori said: You know what, never mind.

When the toilet stopped flushing the faucet continued. The faucet handle was frost-veiled and frigid, as always. On an impulse he pressed his injured hand to it. The deep cold made it feel better for a moment. His wife was now coming down the stairs. They walked to the café. Their younger son protested. Montessori was glad. He did not know how he would explain the hat in his car, which he was sure still sat on the passenger seat. Their younger son grew more and more excited the closer they got to the place, where he had never been.

While they were still a block away, he began shouting: I see him, in the window! I see Josep! In the window!

Montessori said: I think I see him too.

When they reached the place, Montessori almost walked past it. They had repainted the outside a dark, grayish-blue. New, green-check curtains hung in the front windows. A new sign was affixed to the outer wall above the windows. It said: HENRI'S MUSTACHE. Next to the words was an ideographic cartoon. A round hat above a pair of old-fashioned spectacles, and beneath these the two black narrow wings of a mustache.

Mrs. Montessori said: What are you doing? Let's go in.

Montessori made himself smile, made himself walk up and open the door, made himself walk through. They had redone the interior. They had put skylights in. The walls were the same dark gray-blue. On the walls they had photographs of famous mustaches through history. Toulouse-Lautrec, of course. Charlie Chaplin, Cab Calloway, Stalin (no Hitler), David Niven, and Cesar Romero. Others Montessori did not know, including some sort of forest Slav. Plus Salvador Dali on the far end. Josep stood at the counter under the skylight. Next to him was the blonde girl, the one who had been working the day Montessori broke the bathroom mirror. The one who had seen him leave with his bloodied hand. She was looking at Montessori. He put his bandaged hand into his pocket. The bandage snagged on the pocket edge and made the wound start hurting again. Josep had not noticed him yet. Mrs. Montessori strode forward with their younger son, who was grinning and unfolding the drawing he had made.

Josep said: Hey, what a surprise.

His brother said: Look what I made for you.

Josep looked at the picture, smiling broadly. The blonde girl smiled too. She took it and got a roll of tape used to close the white boxes they put baked goods in, and taped it up on the wall behind the register.

Their younger son said: I'm glad I signed it!

A round plumpish face and a round plumpish hat, round plumpish spectacles, a round plumpish mustache. The pencil strokes firm and clear. Mrs. Montessori applauded lightly. Montessori made himself smile again. Kept the smile in place as he ordered. The blonde girl was the one who took his order; Josep got called away to the back. The blonde girl, after meeting Montessori's eyes once, refused to meet them again while he was ordering and paying (though she was otherwise polite and efficient). While he and his wife and younger son sat to eat, Montessori watched the blonde girl (and the drawing). He saw her leaning over to whisper to another employee, an older woman, and then the fourth, a boy who looked about her own age. She did not lean over and whisper to Josep when he returned. Montessori excused himself. He needed to see the men's room. They had replaced the door: the same dark blue gray as the walls. Inside they had reorganized the placement of the sink and the toilet. A quick job, and well-done. The mirror he had broken was no longer there. His hand ached, much worse than before, while he stared into the new one. He did not see anything. No hat and no spectacles. No mustache, and nothing else. Though he stood and looked until his eyes ached from his refusal to blink.

A little knock on the door broke his stare. He opened it and saw his younger son, standing there and smiling.

He said: Mama sent me to find out if something is wrong.

Montessori walked back to the table holding his younger son's hand. In his left. The right ached and screamed. The pain was so bad now it was starting to make Montessori nauseated. He had to cradle it against his side, as if the hand were broken. He felt sweat starting near his hairline and coursing down past his temples, down his neck.

Mrs. Montessori said: Are you alright? You look sick.

Montessori made himself smile again.

He said: no, just a little cold. Or a little hot. I guess I might be coming down with something.

His younger son put his small, warm palm on Montessori's forehead.

He said: Yep, dad definitely has a disease, he's all sweaty!

The blonde girl was leaning and whispering to her colleague again: the older woman. She started looking right at Montessori, quite openly, with a slightly vacant brown gaze. Luckily, his younger son had finished his bagel and was ready to leave. Mrs. Montessori took their younger son to the park. He had soccer practice. Montessori did not like the idea of being alone in the house, but he said nothing, he simply hugged his younger son for longer than usual.

The boy said: Geez, dad, please get better, you're getting me all wet.

Montessori went directly to the backyard when he got home. His hand hurt, the pain welling up and falling away, returning more and more strongly. He could feel his intestines churning and slick, hot saliva filling his mouth. He opened the bandage. He did not know what he expected to see. Bloody pus, white-purple swollen flesh. To smell gangrene. But the wound itself, as it had been for days, was clean. Largely healed except for a thin, decorous scab, the color of dead brick. The flesh to either side – though it caused Montessori unspeakable agony when he prodded it – was neither swollen nor hot. He walked to the bodega (rather than going into his house) and bought some aspirin and a can of seltzer. He walked back to his patio and swallowed two, then four, then six of the pills. If they did not help, he was going to have to go to the emergency room. His primary care physician did not see patients on Saturdays.

His ears buzzed from the aspirin. It was not helping, not at all. He felt hot, syrup-headed, he needed to shit (also from the aspirin). Still, he remained in the chair. Remained in the baking sun. His shirt stuck to his chest. There was a little shadow, a mild shadow. Where was it? In old Señor Periander's open window. He could see it, could see it right from his chair. It was doing nothing. The worst part. Standing, fluttering a little. There was nothing he could reproach it with. He closed his eyes and listened to his own breathing.

It was Old Abel who woke him up. The cat was butting at his wounded hand with his sharp head, batting at the stray threads from the bandage. The renewed, different pain cleared Montessori's head. He got to his feet and started walking. He would walk all the way to the hospital. Old Abel raced back and forth, chirping and yelling, and even followed Montessori a little way into the front yard. Montessori texted his wife, saying he was heading to the ER, but nothing to worry about. Just the hand. He thought it was infected. He knelt down and stroked Old Abel's head with his left hand and looked into the cat's yellow-green eyes.

The hospital, Hokkusai-Metternich, was not far from Montessori's house. He took a cab. He avoided looking in the rearview mirror. At the hospital, he explained his situation to the duty nurse behind the attendance desk.

The nurse said: Has there been any discharge or swelling?

Montessori said: There was swelling but it went down. And never any discharge.

The nurse said: What about fever?

Montessori said: No, just pain.

The nurse was typing, not looking any longer.

He said: Please take your seat, sir, and we will be with you when we can.

Montessori looked around the waiting room once he had gotten back to his seat. The waiting room was mostly full. Despite the air conditioning being on such a high setting it interfered with hearing, the room was still unpleasantly warm. He saw families huddled around children. One had a broken arm, the wrist swollen into a U. Another, a little girl with long braids, had her right foot wrapped in a towel saturated with blood. The little girl was not moving around much; she looked tired. Her mother was rocking and muttering to herself. There were also some single adults present. Montessori saw a squat, bulky man in a black coverall, with a fluffy gray mustache. He was pressing a wadded-up paper towel to his naked scalp. There was a woman with thick black spectacles whose breathing was visibly shallow and irregular. The little sighs she made came through even above the loud air conditioning. He spotted a slumped old man in a brown ball cap. The old man was tearing and tearing at an open, red-purple sore on his neck. A sweet smell filled up the waiting room, along with the air-conditioning noise. Along administrative nothing. You know all about it.

His phone rang. It was his wife. The reception in the waiting room was bad and he could not hear her. He tried texting her but the text failed to send, and the same thing happened when he tried to send an email. The pain in his hand hampered him as he tapped at his phone, and he found himself sick from the pain. More sweat was running down his face, hairline to chin. A soft moaning. Where was that coming from? He realized the nurse was standing right next to him. For a moment he smiled. Were they going to see him now?

The nurse said: Could you please be quiet, sir? You are disturbing the other patients.

Montessori tried to stop whimpering. The pain was harsher and clearer now. His hand felt swollen, inflated. Like the skin was tearing, blood was leaking through. He knew this was impossible, he could see from his fingers and the shape of the bandage that the hand was normal size. The sensation, the pain, kept getting worse. He tried asking the duty nurse for a painkiller. His voice was hoarse and soft.

The nurse said: What was that, sir?

Montessori repeated his request. He struggled to make himself heard over the endless noise of the air conditioner.

The nurse said: If you don't stop making a disturbance, sir, I am going to have to ask you to leave. You must wait your turn like everyone else.

A cool, clerical gaze rested on him. He only saw the woman with thick, black spectacles looking dully in his direction. Montessori sat back down. He shuffled his feet desperately, as a child in pain does. The old man picked at his red purple sore. His brown, round ball cap went on bobbing. The bald man with the fluffy mustache was wiping at his scalp. Something in the corner glinted like a mirror. Montessori had to shut his eyes. He opened them again. He needed to lie down. The chairs here were too narrow and small. Better to get sofas. Montessori fell twice on his way back to the emergency room exit. He stumbled first near the child with the bloody foot and again near the bald man, wiping and wiping. The second time, he heard people running up, heard people shouting. He was on the floor, face pressed against the linoleum. It was cold, scentless. All he saw were feet, moving feet and legs. Amid all the movement one pair stood serene.

He woke up in a cool bed. The room was cool. A window looked out over a concrete inner garden. The pain in his hand was gone. Sitting in a chair across from the bed was Mrs. Montessori. Sitting on her lap was their younger son.

Mrs. Montessori said: You're awake. Right?

Montessori moved his hand around a little. The pain did not return. He was wearing a hard plastic brace that covered the palm and part of the wrist.

Mrs. Montessori said: There was an infection but it was near the bone. So that's why it seemed OK. They drained it and put in drugs and they stitched it up. The hole is so small, though. Just one stitch. And you need the brace for a few days.

When he tried to make a fist, there was a small twinge. That was all.

Mrs. Montessori said: They asked if you'd been behaving strangely. While you were asleep. I told them a little. Sometimes that happens with cases like this. There can be phantom sensations.

His younger son hid his face against his mother's arm. She patted his dark, lustrous hair and stroked his neck. His hair was the precise shade and texture of her own.

Mrs. Montessori said: No, they called them "chimerical experiences." Sorry.

Montessori looked from her to his son, from his son to the small mirror set on the wall near the door. He saw nothing, just a fragment of the window in the opposite wall. He closed his fist once more, again, a third time. Now even the twinge was gone. He was no longer cold, no longer sweating. Nothing leered down or stood nearby.

Mrs. Montessori said: Oh yeah, I almost forgot. You know how the upholsterer was supposed to come?

Montessori nodded.

His younger son said: What's an upholsterer?

Mrs. Montessori said: I got a call from his nephew. He broke his leg skiing. He's not going to be able to make it. The nephew said we should try to find someone else.

Montessori didn't answer. He kept his eyes on the mirror. He thought he might have seen something.

His younger son said, again: What's an upholsterer?

At home, it was as if the fever and injury had never occurred. He sat in the kitchen while his wife played catch with their younger son in the backyard. No faucet turned on in the bathroom, no toilet flushed. He joined them, bringing a beer for his wife and a bottle of lemonade for his son. He saw nothing in Señor Periander's upstairs window. It was closed, the curtain still. Not a gleam or a glimpse. The sofa, too, had lost its stale, damp smell. Montessori did not sniff it in the presence of his wife or sons. He took the risk when he was alone. The upholstery, despite its age, smelled as though it had just been laundered. It felt less stiff and brittle, as well, and the wood of the frame sang less loudly.

At his office, he saw no more glimpses or gleams in the mirror. Nothing distracted him during meetings, or spun a hat while he explained the phase of the project. When he went to get lunch at the cafe on the weekends, or a day he happened to be home, he saw nothing of any kind. The blonde girl, Josep's school friend, did not look at him, did not lean toward her colleagues and mumble into their ears. True, Old Abel retained his dislike of the sofa. He still refused to climb on it, to play under it, and if their younger son tried to carry him over to it, he trilled in protest and wriggled free. Montessori knew animals are more sensitive than humans are.

Above all, despite his pain getting better, despite his more restful nights, Montessori felt tired. The sofa had been in their house for less than a month, and he felt far more tired than he had even when their older son was a baby and staying awake through the night, when he had also been getting his business through its first months. His exhaustion did not prevent him from working or amusing his wife, from playing with his younger son and speaking to Josep. It dragged him down more and more quickly every night and made climbing out of bed more difficult in the morning. During the day, he moved more slowly and spoke more slowly, even when the lethargy annoyed or frustrated him. At times it felt (only a little) like he was not the master of his own limbs, his own rubbery mouth. As if his hand had gone numb. Or as if he had just come back from the dentist. It also reminded him of taking acid, which he had always deeply disliked.

A few days into his lethargy, Montessori got a phone call from the haulers. The one he had set up a time to take the sofa away with. The day had arrived. Montessori had been so distracted he failed to remember, and when the company called him he assumed it was some new effort on the part of a certain gentleman. No: there were no problems or issues, no requests for fees or documents. The sales rep cited the day and time and asked if Montessori wanted to confirm.

Montessori hesitated.

The sales rep spoke again: Sir, did you want to confirm?

He felt his mouth go rubbery, his lips a little numb. He licked them once, twice, gulped down saliva. A light tickle of pain in his hand.

The sales rep said: Sir, this is the last opening we have for some time, and there are other potential customers who might want it if you don't.

Montessori said: For how long?

Speaking relieved the numbness a little. The pain got worse and worse. Not as bad as it had been before but still pretty bad. A high, strumming throb.

The sales rep said: For some time, sir.

Montessori gulped down more air and saliva.

He said: We don't need the pickup. The situation has changed a little bit over here.

The sales rep said: Are you sure, sir?

The pain was humming and stinging now. So badly Montessori had to close his fist.

Montessori said: Yes, I'm sure. I appreciate your call.

The sales rep hung up without saying another word. At once, the pain in Montessori's hand vanished. The numbness in his lips had gone as well. He was even feeling a little less tired. He kept expecting the pain to return. It did not. That seemed impossible to Montessori. Could it all be so crude and simple? Why not?

By the time he started his drive home, he felt almost relieved. The sofa affair was taken care of, his hand pain was gone. The lethargy kept on flowing out of him. He reached his driveway feeling more awake than when he had left it. He saw through the living room window the dining room table. Wine gleamed in a decanter. Josep was setting out forks while his younger son folded napkins. He heard his wife's voice drifting out as he walked from the car through his front door. He looked right at the sofa as he crossed the living room. Even brushed some fluffy lint off the bowed part in its back, let his hand linger on the ridged, eroded nap of the upholstery. It felt warmish, almost like the hide of a dog beneath the pelt.

The smell of the roast chicken his wife brought to the table made him salivate. He found he was more awake, that all his lethargy had vanished. His mouth no longer felt rubbery at all. He drank most of the carafe of wine as he ate, opened another bottle, poured for his wife, held her warm, dry hand on top of the table. Josep recounted his first week on the job. How he liked the manager and was earning a lot of tips.

Their younger son said: I am doing well at my job too. But my partner – you know, this kid they make me work with – well, he died of rabies.

Montessori fixed ice cream sundaes for dessert. They boys ate them and went to play soccer in the backyard. He and his wife had more wine and some lemon sorbet. His wife had become lactose intolerant after Josep was born. The second bottle was almost gone when Montessori heard his younger son scream. He glanced at his wife and trotted outside. The boys must have gotten in a fight. They sometimes did when they played soccer, because Josep was far more skilled and strong and he often got caught up in the game and forgot to go easy on his brother. As he reached the doorway Montessori heard Josep say: What the fuck.

He came out into the yard. He saw the boys standing still. Or no, only Josep was standing. His younger son was kneeling in the grass near the fencepost that formed one side of the goal (it and its twin had now-faded orange ribbons tied around them). He was moving back and forth on his knees and weeping. The tears on his face glowed with light from the streetlamp.

Josep said: Sorry for saying fuck, dad.

Montessori said: What happened? Did he hurt himself?

Josep said: You better look.

His younger son said: Papa, no, no, papa.

His voice rose to a screech and then into shrill silence. His tears flowed and he swayed more and more deeply. Montessori saw black, lustrous streaks on his arms: blood. He rushed close and lifted the boy, checking his arms and torso for wounds.

His younger son said: No, no – look.

He pointed to the fence. At the bottom of the goalpost was a dark, crushed pile. Cloth? Garbage? He turned on his phone flashlight.

Old Abel. The light caught in his dull eyes. His small body quivered once. The legs looked broken. His fur and pelt were torn across his belly and sides. The cuts were deep enough to expose his viscera and the white of his ribs. The cat was still breathing. Sticky blood had stiffened already in the fur around the wounds. A rank smell rose, urine. Montessori felt ill. There was no pain in his hand, no numbness in his mouth. He gathered his younger son into his arms and rocked him while he cried. The tears were scalding on his neck. Josep's eyes gleamed in the light from the streetlamp. Mrs. Montessori came out and saw them.

She said: What's the matter? What happened?

Josep pointed. Mrs. Montessori did not see.

Montessori said: It's Abel. Something tore him up.

His younger son entered a new paroxysm. Montessori held him tighter. Mrs. Montessori was gasping now, attempting to lift the small body. The black, lustrous smears appeared on her hands and gleamed. Montessori got a trowel from the garage. He dug a deep, short trench as the boys and his wife watched. His younger son ran off, still weeping, and then came back with a pink blanket. It had been his as a baby. He and Josep wrapped the small body, no longer quivering, in the blanket. Montessori lowered it into the trench and covered it up. His younger son was kneeling and rocking, his mouth moving. Montessori could not understand what the boy was saying.

After they managed to get the boys to sleep – Josep demanded that they call the police and his brother wept and wept – Mrs. Montessori took a long shower. Montessori's eyes kept slipping shut, his mouth kept slipping open. He pressed and pressed at his hand. Still no pain. He chewed on the inside of his cheeks and slapped himself lightly to stay awake. Mrs. Montessori finished showering. She came and sat on the edge of the bed, in her towel, slumping slightly. As always, Montessori felt a deep physical surge at the sight of her bare legs, bare arms and shoulders, trim breasts under the towel. For a long time all he heard was the squeaking of the towel against her hair.

She said: Do you think it was a raccoon?

Montessori said: I don't know.

Mrs. Montessori was crying again, a little. She wiped at her eyes with the second towel. She lay down next to Montessori, still damp, with her back to him. He tucked an arm under her head and she began to cry much harder into his elbow crook.

Montessori said: We can call animal control tomorrow.

In the morning, he found his younger son kneeling out by the grave of Old Abel. The earth looked raw and black. The boy had his hand on the low, scar-like mound. Montessori went out and squatted down next to him. The boy, he saw, had glued two popsicle sticks together, each colored green, in the shape of an equilateral cross, and pushed the lower arm into the mound. Around the upper arm, the boy had hung Old Abel's collar from when he was a kitten, which he had outgrown years before. Where the boy had found it, Montessori had no idea. His wife called animal control after Josep had gone to work and their younger son had started his soccer camp for the day.

She said: No, I did not see it happen. It must have been a raccoon. Or a dog. A loose dog.

Montessori did not hear what the person on the other end said. His wife screamed: well, fuck you, then!

She threw her phone across the kitchen table. It landed in the sink with a musical clang (and rustle). She slumped against the wall with her hands covering her face. Montessori rose and embraced her. She was weeping again, lightly and silently, though Old Abel had been his cat. Montessori could tell her. She might not believe him. She might blame him. But she would listen. Now, she would listen. He remembered the lustrous blood on his son's thin arms and how light his son's body had felt in his own arms. The words were in his mouth, along with the air and saliva. He said nothing. There was a tiny twinge of pain in his hand, which soon vanished.

Josep and their younger son were both in favor of getting a new cat right away. Mrs. Montessori wanted to wait for a while, and Montessori agreed that was best. He expected the boys to make a big fuss but they did not. Again, as they discussed the possible new cat, there was a tiny twinge of pain in his hand. It was barely there, only a moment. Montessori still felt it. That night, he felt the cool, clerical gaze upon him. That also only rested on his back for a moment but he still knew it had happened.

The boys moved their soccer goal out of respect for the grave. Montessori was happy to see that only two nights went by before they were playing again. It was hard, too, for Montessori to go back to sitting out there at first. The patio chairs were arranged so that the grave was right in his sightline. He decided that, no matter the rules, he was not going to be forbidden from his own yard. The small sickness he felt when he thought about the cat's last moments he forced himself to conquer. Mrs. Montessori would join him, sit close enough to hold his (pain-free) right hand. Her gaze kept falling to the grave, her face closing a little. The small metal disk on the collar would gleam blankly in reflected light, like a solitary eye. Montessori found that he had to fight back the urge to tell her at times when they were sitting side by side in the dusk. Every time he started to speak, there was a little twinge. Or not even a twinge, just a sensation. He said nothing about it. They just went on holding hands and watching the boys play.

Still, Montessori liked to go out by himself in the yard. Just to make sure. Late at night he'd walk around the edge, stop and pay his respects to the grave, and peer over the fence into the yards to either side. In the morning he had coffee out there and read his newspaper, weekend and weekday alike. One weekend morning, after his wife had gone out to buy groceries, Josep had left for his job, and their younger son had gone to an all-day birthday party, he was sitting alone and staring at the now-dulling metal of the cat tag. The collar was gray, it had previously been pale blue. Was it time to take it off? He could explain to the boys that this way they'd always have a memento of Old Abel. Before he could properly think up how, he heard a sound. Deep, dull, regular. Like the noise of a woodpecker, slowed down, magnified.

It was coming from out front. He walked out to see and he found a man in a green coverall suit pounding a tall, rectangular wooden post into the front yard of Señor Periander. The man was using a rubber-topped mallet. He was breathing hard with the effort, and sweat covered his forehead, but he was smiling. He had a large mole near his mouth that resembled a fly. Bristly, as if iridescent. Montessori recognized him. He did not even feel a shock of surprise. It was the desk man, the smiling desk man. The corporate campus parking lot security guard He wiped his forehead with his sleeve and looked up at Montessori.

The man said: You look familiar.

Montessori said: Yes. We've met before. A couple of times.

The man lifted his mallet.

He said: That's right. I remember now. Turns out being a desk worker at a dry-cleaning products company doesn't pay well either.

He smashed the mallet down on the flat top of the post. It sank another two inches into the earth. The man was much stronger than his short, rattish build suggested. Now he took a wooden dowel out from the green canvas bag at his feet and, with a much smaller hammer taken from the same bag, tapped it into a pole in the post's side. Montessori was seized with a sudden and absurd fear: Señor Periander had died and this was his memorial, they were going to bury him in the front lawn. But there was only one dowel, not the two needed for a cross. When it was secure, the mallet worker took a flat plastic placard from the bag and strapped it to the dowel through two holes near the top, so that it swung freely in the wind. A FOR SALE sign. The selling agency was called Heseltine Melamed.

The mallet worker said: There's a real shortage of high-paying jobs.

He stood and looked at the sign, holding the mallet against his hip.

Then he said: I'm not supposed to do this, but maybe you can help me out.

Montessori said: What do you mean?

The mallet worker said: If I lend you this mallet, can you keep an eye on the sign? I'd do it myself but I have other engagements. If the wind moves the sign, knocks it over, can you try and hammer it back into place?

Montessori was so surprised by this request that he found himself smiling, which the mallet worker took as an assent. He tossed the mallet at Montessori's feet and picked up the rest of his things.

He said: It's easy, just hit straight down. You have to hit harder than you think. This old post can take it, don't worry.

Montessori lifted the mallet. It was heavy. He was expecting pain when he picked it up. He felt nothing. The handle was damp and warm from the man's hand.

The mallet worker said: Remember, harder than you think. A lot harder.

He was already loading his other tools back into his green canvas bag and walking away, wearing a somnolent smile. Montessori said nothing in response, only nodded. He and his wife and sons talked about the new neighbors they would eventually have that night at dinner.

Their younger son said: And what if it's another kid? What am I supposed to do then?

Montessori smiled and said: I think it's going to be fine.

His wife and sons went on discussing the neighbors for the rest of the meal. His younger son had a lot of trouble that night. At first he flopped back and forth and sighed, then he began to rotate, to twirl up the bedclothes. Montessori was sitting in the darkness, in the boy's little chair, but there was just enough light for him to see.

Finally his younger son sat up and said: Seriously, dad. What if it's another kid?

Montessori said: Maybe you could be friends.

His younger son said: That's too risky!

Montessori said: Why is it risky?

His younger son said: Because what if the kid tells me to go to?

Montessori took his younger son on his lap and held him. That usually helped the boy when he had these difficulties. The boy kept muttering about how risky this "new neighbor kid" was going to be. As tired as Montessori was – remember that his general exhaustion had not fully left him – he found he had to fight back chuckles. Eventually the boy began to snore lightly, his warm breath touching the back of Montessori's right hand. Montessori lightly dropped him in his bed and left the room. His younger son woke up again half an hour later. He blinked and shifted from foot to foot in the light of Montessori's bed-side lamp.

Montessori said: What's the matter?

His younger son shrugged and stuck out his hand. Montessori suspected the boy was still not fully awake.

Montessori said: What's the matter? What is it?

Again the boy shrugged and held up his arms. Montessori lifted him and carried him back over to the chair. He did not shut off the light this time. He suspected the boy would fall fully back asleep with it on. Soon enough, the boy did. His small body took on the usual heaviness of sleep, real sleep, as Montessori lowered him again into the bed and tucked the blanket over him. He returned to bed and picked up the book he had been reading. It was about a neurologist, a famous British neurologist named Hartley Melville (and in fact he had been reading it for a long time, since before his troubles began). He fell asleep looking at a picture of this British man, with his steely mustache and steely spectacles, the steely brim of his somber homburg.

What woke him was the cool clerical gaze. At least that's what it felt like. As he hurled himself over in bed, he realized that his younger son was standing there. Right next to the bed. Standing rigidly, as if at attention. Eyes open, and staring down at him. His face looked pale, blank in the moonlight and his dark eyes seemed much darker.

Montessori said: Are you alright?

His younger son said nothing, only went on staring. His eyes shone as blank as lenses, and he swayed a little. Mrs. Montessori went on snoring. Montessori stroked his son's forehead, tugged on his shoulder. The boy's muscles felt rigid, trembling a little. Even the muscles of his jaw felt hard and locked. His skin was not hot, in fact it was slightly clammy, and his breath came rapidly and shallowly. He tried to pick the boy up. His body was so stiff, so unyielding, that Montessori could not find a grip other than around his legs. The boy stayed totally upright while Montessori carried him back to his room, and stretched out ramrod stiff once he had laid him back in his bed. He did not speak to Montessori or look at him. Yes, Montessori knew all the possibilities. It could be epilepsy, some new form of epilepsy (the boy was not epileptic). Or it could be a nightmare, a waking nightmare, or sleep paralysis (the boy was not asleep).

Despite these possibilities, he knew in fact what it was.

Montessori sat in his younger son's desk chair. The boy lay as he had left him, unmoving. He was breathing, still fast and shallow. Montessori felt a sick panic rising in him. He got out of the chair and began to pace back and forth. He kept looking at his younger son, immobile, the moonlight shining on his blank, lens-like eyes. Montessori tried again to wake the boy. He knelt by his bed, stroked his chest and crooned into his ear. No response at all. The high, almost whining respiration. The muscles still rigid and trembling. At least he had to show his wife. First the cat and now this. It took time to wake her. He explained what he had seen and he saw her face contract with fear in the moonlight. They rushed back to their younger son's room.

As soon as they entered, Montessori heard a different respiration. Not the labored, shrillish sound from before but an even, peaceful breathing. He saw that his son was no longer rigid, but lying (as usual) with his arms tangled up and mouth open. His skin, when Montessori felt it, was no longer clammy but smooth and warm.

Mrs. Montessori yawned and said: What was it.

Montessori said: I don't know. He was rigid, like he was having a seizure.

His wife said: Poor guy.

Montessori said: Yeah, I'll sit up with him for a while.

He watched his son for one hour, two. In the cool moonlight. The sick fear never left him. He expected the boy to go stiff again, rise up with his hieratic posture, open the blank eyes. Instead, he flopped back and forth, smiled a soft smile, babbled a little, chewed air like a fish.

In the morning, the boy was fine. He did not mention anything about the previous night and he did not even seem tired.

He said: I decided it isn't that risky. If a kid moves in next door. Even if he tells me to go right to hell.

Montessori still felt afraid. He tried to examine the boy from across the table. His eyes looked normal, his muscle movement looked normal. There was no trace of rigidity, nothing lens-like, nothing blank in his gaze. He embraced his younger son for a long time before taking him to the corner for the soccer camp bus and again when the bus arrived. Josep had an early shift at Henri's Mustache; Montessori passed him on his way back to the house. Mrs. Montessori was gone already, out for a run, when he got home. He sat for a while in the kitchen, to see whether there would be toilet and faucet sounds from the first-floor bathroom. He heard nothing, just the modest creaking of the joists within the walls. He tried to perform one of his mirror and window checks. His fear, which had gotten worse and worse, made him half-hearted, he found he was wandering back and forth, knees shaking a little, and soon gave up.

Out in the yard, where Montessori went to finish his coffee and try to relax, it was even worse. Because there, no matter where he was, the sun glinted off the dull, blank eye of the cat collar tag hung on the cross. The small, torn body, and the dark lustrous blood. His own breathing was now fast and shallow. A dense, slimy sweat covered his back, his feet, his neck. He tried forcing himself to sit down in the deck chair, but could not stay seated. He tried to call his wife – not to tell her, just to talk. He felt that feathery sensation against his right hand, and the longer he contemplated calling her the longer it built and increased. A loud, crisp noise broke into his fear and pain.

A door had opened and shut. Montessori saw a shadow move across the window of Señor Periander's living room, and ran to the fence, climbed over.

There it was, wavering away, moving within the gray depth of the room. He watched, still shaking a little. The shadow came back. It was a tall, angular woman in jeans and a white shirt. She was walking through the living room, holding a clipboard.

A large, red birthmark covered her face beneath her left eye. Montessori realized this must be the realtor selling the house. His sudden relief made him feel almost nauseated. The realtor saw him and rushed through the rear door˙before he could get back over the fence.

The realtor said: Excuse me, this is private property.

Montessori said: Señor Periander was a friend of mine and I thought someone had broken into his house.

The realtor said: Why would you think that, given the sign out front?

Montessori said: You never know what will happen.

She looked at him, and it seemed to Montessori that her inflamed birthmark (the kind called hemangioma) grew more inflamed, breathing with pompous outrage. Montessori did not move.

The realtor said: We appreciate your efforts but we've got it all under control over here.

She went back inside. Montessori climbed over the fence. He saw her out of the corner of his eye for the rest of the morning, walking back and forth, taking measurements in the garden. She even went out on the roof. She had put on a baseball cap and sunglasses and was examining the slate roof tiles. She used a small hammer to tap at them, her ear close to the roof surface. The sofa was giving off a smell again. The faintest smell yet. So faint Montessori had to struggle to find it. Find it he did, every time. Snuffling and snorting. He recalled his younger's son's blank eyes. The blank eye of the cat collar tag shining away in the golden sunlight.

Despite his sick fear, both Josep and Montessori's younger son arrived home without any incident. His younger son was covered with mud. Apparently, the fire department had opened a hydrant near the soccer camp field and he and his campmates had spent the day playing in the water and dirt.

Josep sat in the kitchen drinking seltzer.

He said: One of the managers is leaving and they are going to promote me to manager trainee.

Mrs. Montessori, who had returned from her run, said: You'll be running the place soon!

Their younger son wanted steak for dinner. Montessori prepared the grill. He piled up the coal in the metal lighting cylinder and stuffed newspaper into the hollow under it. He lit the paper. The flame licked and spread. He waited until it was covered with gray ash. Mrs. Montessori brought the steaks out. He pulled his hand away before she saw him holding it in place above the fire. Their younger son also wanted to eat outside, and everyone else backed up this desire. Montessori was usually happy to eat in the backyard. This time the eye of the cat collar tag gave off a dull light. The light touched the back of his neck. It was not a cool, clerical gaze. It distracted him all the same. Like a mustache, flapping away in a gentle breeze. The grill was still hot. He could see the air distorted above it. What if he pressed his hand, his right hand, hard down onto the grill bars – what then?

That night Montessori prepared himself for another episode with his younger son. He read to the boy for a long time, as long as he wanted. He pulled down his window shade to keep the room dark. When the boy had fallen asleep, he fixed a cup of strong tea and sat erect in bed reading. He read a detective novel, BUDAPEST GAMBIT (featuring the amazing, unkillable Inspector Andric) to keep himself alert and awake. He noticed, though he had read the book before, that the lithograph-style illustrations showed Andric with a bowler and spectacles (no mustache), and he braced himself still harder. At two in the morning, all was quiet. He snuck down the hall. Stood at his younger son's door. Listened for his breath. It was deep, calm. He opened the door and saw the boy's relaxed body, watched his chest evenly rise and fall.

Montessori slept well after that. He woke up later than usual. He urinated, brushed his teeth. He went to check on his younger son. He felt a little sick, but he forced himself to open the door.

The boy was not in his bed.

The bed was made, cleanly and tightly. The boy was not in it. Montessori felt himself getting dizzier and dizzier. He leaned against the doorjamb. He ran downstairs. First thing to do: Call the police and all the boy's friends. Get out in the car and start looking. He found he was almost hyperventilating, that his vision was blurring. As he got downstairs, he stopped running. His younger son was on the sofa. Curled up near the end. He was small enough to fit on it with room to spare. He was breathing as he had the previous night, sweetly and deeply. He was even smiling in his sleep, a warm friendly smile. Montessori ran into the living room. His younger son's eyes slipped open and he sat up. He smiled even more broadly when he saw Montessori.

He said: Papa!

Then he jumped up and ran to hug Montessori, who got down on his knees to embrace the boy. He forced his breathing to slow down.

His younger son said: Why are you so sweaty?

Montessori said: It's hot upstairs.

His younger son said: I can stand by your bed and throw ice cubes on you next time.

That morning, once the boys had gone, Montessori saw on his way to the office that the FOR SALE sign in Señor Periander's yard had fallen over during the night. There had been no wind, no storm. Montessori almost walked past and left it there. He stopped, then rushed back inside and into his basement and retrieved the rubber mallet. He swung awkwardly at first.After four attempts found his rhythm. The signpost slid back into the soft, fragrant earth. He put the mallet back, wiped away his sweat, and went to work.

The transactional phase had begun, and there was plenty to do at the office. Montessori directed his senior evaluators and modelers to finalize their projections; he had the chief counsel examine the contracts, which had just arrived the previous day. This activity, frantic but benign and familiar, permitted Montessori some peace during the day. Only once or twice did he feel a feather touch on his hand, and not one single time did he see any glimpses in mirrors, chairs or elsewhere. Toward the end of the day, the assistant researcher came into Montessori's office. She was carrying a white folder and she had bluish semicircles on the skin under her eyes. Her skin was the color of milk.

She said: We found something on that filing request you made, a while back.

Montessori said: What do you mean?

She gave him the folder.

She said: You were looking for any filings under the name Meervermesser.

The folder held only a few papers. Montessori was surprised not to have seen them before. They outlined a long-expired charter for a company that had incorporated to exploit New York's industrial garnet resources, under the name I. Meervermesser. The handwriting (the form had been hand-filled, not typed) was almost illegible. The strokes firm and faint, once black, now reddish, growing more and more gold. The papers included some facsimile photographs of the proposed zone of exploitation. A vacant field, huge and wide, backed by low, moronic crags. A river crossed by a wooden, irregular footbridge bounded one edge. Its shadow blackened a section of the long shingle covered with leprous stones. Standing in the field, near the bridge, was a short figure. The photograph blurry and the image inexact. It seemed to Montessori that the figure wore (at least) a roundish, plumpish hat. More than that? Hard to say. He brought the file home with him and put the photograph up on the refrigerator door next to the drawing his younger son had made. From even a few feet away the smeary figure seemed to be only an agglomeration of earth or stones, a fat dwarfish bush. Close up it appeared. A human, a plump human. With a human's unique, stupidly arrogant stance.

Josep asked at dinner: What is that a picture of?

Montessori said: You know, I am really not sure.

His younger son said: I like it, it looks like there's a secret cave. Inside the cave you could find a beach.

Mrs. Montessori said: If there was a beach inside a cave, I assure you I would be a return customer.

Their younger son said: You don't have to pay to go to the beach, mama.

For a moment, Montessori thought he heard the sound of the downstairs bathroom toilet flushing and the faucet hissing. It was simply some sound from outdoors, a vacant wind passing by. Josep went out after dinner. He had to meet a friend. Montessori's younger son fell asleep on the sofa while reading a comic book. Montessori carried him upstairs. The boy stayed warm and limp as Montessori tucked him in. He and Mrs. Montessori stood in the doorway of his room for a while, watching him. The faint stale smell drifted up and entered Montessori's nose, then it vanished.

Mrs. Montessori said: I think Josep is meeting his little girlfriend. I think it's that girl from the cafe.

Montessori said: You know what? We should go on vacation.

His wife said: This is sudden.

Montessori said: To celebrate my recovery.

His wife smiled a little. She wrinkled her nose.

She said: I hope not to the beach, we go there all the time.

Montessori said: I was thinking we could rent a place for a while. Upstate. Go to the mountains.

Mrs. Montessori said: Since when do you propose last-minute vacations?

Montessori said: It's been a stressful summer.

They began the planning right away. It was already July and they needed to move quickly. Montessori consulted Josep and his younger son. Both children were in favor of a vacation. Josep wanted to go to the beach and his younger son wanted to go "to a forest" (by which Montessori thought he meant somewhere upstate). Josep gave up his objections after not too much arguing. He admitted he was also a little tired of the beach. Montessori began looking. There were more open places than he had expected, but most of them were shitty. He would show his family a collection of three or four every night, but they never found anyone compelling enough to book. He persevered. The transaction phase would close in three weeks and he wanted to leave town right afterwards. For a long time. He hoped the rest of the summer. After six days, he found a place. It was big: five bedrooms, two screened porches. It was deep in the woods but not too far from a town. It had a long, wide pool, a grill, dozens of acres of forest and also grass fields. The property enclosed a stream that flowed between clean, grassy banks. There was a henhouse with chickens from which you could collect fresh eggs. His wife and younger son, when they saw the photos, decided the place was perfect. Josep praised it and said how excited he was to go.

The day after Montessori had started to arrange the departure itself – letting his subordinates know, setting up a mail hold, locating the nearest grocery and liquor stores to the rental – he found as he was leaving for work one morning the realtor pulling the FOR SALE sign out of Señor Periander's front lawn. She was wearing a black business suit despite the heavy, damp weather. Her heels had left two irregular series of holes in the grass. She pulled it out with what seemed to Montessori no effort. He thought of the mallet among his tools in the basement. What if he ran and got it and hammered the post back in as she watched? This idea insisted on itself even as Montessori saw the realtor carry the sign to her car and throw it in the backseat. She drove off. Montessori crouched on the lawn and tried to fill in the hole the signpost had made. He stayed there until the dew had soaked the cuffs of his pants.

Soon, more and more preparations for the new neighbors began. One morning a brown panel truck pulled up and four men in white coveralls came out. They carried tool boxes with them; one steered a hand cart on which planks and joists tied in bundles were piled. They worked all day, even though it was a Saturday, and the thumping and pounding continued into the evening. Montessori's younger son tried to watch what the workers were doing, first by standing on the sidewalk and staring though the front door and then – after one slammed it shut – by watching through the living room windows from his own yard.

The contractors were not the only workers who came. One morning two women, also in white coveralls, parked a green SUV in front of the house and came out with large plastic canisters to which gun-like nozzles were attached via long hoses. They worked all day as well, and the sweet stink from their chemicals drifted over into Montessori's house. There was even a roofer. Montessori's whole family watched him work. He was old, he had fluffy white hair and a huge mustache, as well as goggle-like glasses. He was chubby, too, round and plumpish, and Montessori watched him cross and recross the pointed gray roof with delicacy and ease, as simply and surely as if he had been striding along the sidewalk. He carried his tools in a blue pouch attached to his belt, and he knelt down to check one roof tile or another. Every time he moved his head up or down, left or right, the sun flashed dazzlingly off his glasses. They went white, blazing, and these pinpoints left bright, fading traces when Montessori closed his eyes for a rest.

Neither he nor his wife had seen any death notices for Señor Periander. Montessori had never made more than perfunctory efforts to find out what had happened after he had been taken away in the ambulance. Whether the old man was dead, alive. Montessori assumed he was dead, since the house had clearly been sold. His wife argued it didn't mean necessarily that: they might have put him in a home. She did not specify who "they" were.

She said:Aafter all, someone comes by and goes in and out of the house even when they're not working. I've seen him. Must be his son, I think.

Montessori said: What do you mean.

His right hand was curling and tightening. He kept calm.

His wife said: Some guy comes in, even late at night or early in the morning. He kind of putters around for a while. I can see his shadow moving around. Has to be his son, right?

Montessori said: I certainly hope so.

He did not ask for any details of the visitor's appearance. His wife did not offer any.

There were other workers. A yard maintenance team came and cut the grass front and back and pruned the dead branches from an elm hanging down near the roof. A cleaning service arrived to clean the inside of the house and the windows. The men power-washed the sidewalk, driveway, and garden path, as well as the painted outer walls of the garage. A piano company came as well, to deliver a new instrument. It was gleaming and black, and arrived in a wooden truss, on its side, to fit through the front door. Once it was in the house, someone started to test the keys. They played arpeggio after arpeggio and then some sort of curtailed fugue. The music drifted into Montessori's house just as the chemical smell from the exterminators had.

His younger son said: Can we get a piano? I'm already pretty good at playing it.

Mrs. Montessori said: It's something we can discuss later.

Montessori was about to speak, to say it was certainly a possibility. That sudden sensation brushed his hand. To his alarm, it continued to grow, to expand. He was suddenly sweating with the effort of not crying out.

They were due to leave the next day. Everyone woke up early to finish packing. Montessori and his wife brought two suitcases, Josep one. His brother had packed four suitcases, Montessori discovered. Mrs. Montessori told him to pack more lightly. He discarded everything except for a box of markers and some books.

He said: I can just wash the clothes I have on every day.

As they were preparing to load up their car, Montessori saw a large white moving van coming down the street. He recognized the logo from far away. HERAKLITOS MOVERS. Blue wide letters on the white panel, which was astonishingly clean.

Mrs. Montessori said: We should wait a minute, introduce ourselves.

But the new neighbors were not in the truck, they found, and did not come even after the movers had started unloading. They brought out boxes of books, lamps, and what looked to Montessori like an unplugged wine refrigerator. The boys watched for a while. It became clear the neighbors themselves were not going to show up. Mrs. Montessori got in the car. Montessori followed her and turned on the engine. As he checked the mirror to back down the driveway, he forced back a cry. The movers were carrying in a couch, one holding up each end. It was their couch, the dead couch. The cuts were the same as in the photo the cop had shone them, the stains from the weather. The grayed, dirty wings and horns of white stuffing protruded from the same places in the same shapes. One of the movers was looking right at Montessori. Eye to eye, in the mirror.

Montessori sped off before anyone else in his family noticed the couch. Josep and his brother roared and cheered.

The drive was easy. The traffic getting through the city was not too bad. Montessori had taken trips where crossing Manhattan took almost as long as going the remaining distance. No traffic on the highway either. Montessori found himself almost an hour ahead of schedule. Mrs. Montessori asked if they could stop somewhere: she needed to use the bathroom and get a snack. They found a rest stop and Montessori sat with the boys while she headed inside. After she came out, he realized he needed to urinate as well. The place itself was small and dingy. A low brick building with white tiled walls and floor. There was a shop to get coffee and another to get fried chicken, as well as a drugstore with newspapers, candy, soda, and chips. The signs for the men's room seemed to lead out of the building again, however, and as Montessori followed them he saw a small annex in the waste field behind the main building. He crossed the dry grass to it and was about to enter when he stopped.

There was a crude wooden figure, a carved and painted flat board, propped on stakes driven into a bare patch of the field. A man in an old-fashioned suit, crooking his thumb at the annex. On his head a round hat, across his walleyed gaze black, irregular spectacles had been painted. Above the thick upper lip a painted, gray and extravagant mustache.

From the mouth beneath the mustache a wooden speech bubble expanded: THIS WAY FOR THE FACILITIES, GENTS!

Near the end of the trip, they passed through the town of Plataea, the nearest one to the rented house. The road out of Plataea led up into the woods, off the highway, and soon Montessori found himself driving on roads barely paved among overhanging trees. The light filtered, golden-green, through the leaves. The dense, tannic smell of the forest filled up the car. They reached the house, which looked even larger and bluer than in the rental listing photos. Josep and his brother rushed out of the car and up onto the porch. Montessori began to haul the bags out of the trunk. The house was cool and quiet. The loudest sound was the subtle, musical rustling of the pool water as it circulated. Both boys climbed in as soon as they could get their suits on.

They spent the afternoon swimming. Mrs. Montessori drank almost a whole bottle of wine. Montessori restricted himself to a single beer, which he nursed while he grilled hamburgers and hot dogs. The boys gamboled and shouted, splashed around. He watched them in the fading light, in the warm dusk. The yellow christmas lights strung up along the side of the house and the pergola by the side of the pool appeared as dancing points in the water. Josep found a switch near the patio door that turned on lights set in the pool walls, and these provided a round, slightly fungal light.

Montessori slept deeply that night. So did his wife and his sons. The night was black, utterly green-black. The sawing sound of crickets and the liquid calls of birds (Montessori inaccurately thought of them as nightjars). That's it. The boys slept late, both of them. In the morning Mrs. Montessori had a work call, and she drove into town to take it at a coffee shop. The boys went in the pool again and Montessori sat with his copy of BUDAPEST GAMBIT and read in a deck chair next to the pool. He had brought the next book in the series, which had just come out, to read when he finished. As the sun got higher and higher, a small visual annoyance began to distract Montessori. A bright, hard, fragment of light in the brush just beyond the pool. No matter how he turned his head it still broke into his vision. He was about to move to another deck chair. Instead – feeling a sudden, vertiginous illness – he slipped on his sandals and walked through the gate in the deer fence into the brush beyond the pool edge.

The brush scraped and cut his legs a little as he forced his way through it. It was harder to spot the bright fragment now that he was standing up and walking towards it. By swiveling his head he was able to locate it. In a small, clear patch just out of direct sight of the pool edge, he found it. The clumsy cross driven into the earth, the now-grayed nylon collar hanging from its uppermost arm, and the dull, bright collar tag with the words OLD ABEL incised. Montessori felt an urge to tear the cross from the ground, to dig through the leaves and sticks and into the dirt, down and down. To see, to really see. He walked over to the pool, where he dangled his feet in the water and kept his back to the woods.

Mrs. Montessori was back from the coffee shop much later than Montessori had expected. It was mid-afternoon, in fact. He was on the porch and he saw even as she pulled in with the car that she had a nervous grin on her face.

She got out and said: I have a surprise for you!

Then she opened the trunk of the car and, with some difficulty, lugged out a large, squat, cylindrical object wrapped in brown paper. Montessori took it from her and carried it into the house as the boys followed and Mrs. Montessori darted ahead. The object was top-heavy, and he almost stumbled as he guided it through the narrow front hall. He got it into the living room floor and caught his breath. The boys gathered beside him. Josep reached out to rip the paper.

Mrs. Montessori said: No, let papa do it, it's mostly for him.

Montessori tore a strip from the top. A stale, damp smell rose up. He kept tearing. The paper was tough and fibrous, and well-taped in place. At last he denuded the object. It was an ottoman, plump and round, round and plump. The upholstery, straining against bumptious bone buttons, was a precise match for the sofa. Green and yellow stripes.

Josep said: Wow, mom, that's amazing, where did you find it?

Mrs. Montessori said: There's a shop in town, and this was in the window. I had to buy it.

Montessori said: I think that's incredible.

The stale, damp smell was getting stronger. He ran his hand over the upholstery. It felt clean, hardly worn. The ottoman was in superb condition and the smell had to be chimerical.

Mrs. Montessori said: Do you want to try it out?

She pushed the ottoman in front of the couch in the living room. Montessori hurried to sit down and stretch out his legs.

Montessori said: It's perfect.

His younger son said: Wait, papa!

Then he ran outside to fetch BUDAPEST GAMBIT and brought it back to Montessori, who sat and read while his wife and sons watched. The ottoman was comfortable. It was exactly the right height for Montessori's legs to remain at full relaxation. The cushion on top was full without being too hard, and relaxed without being too soft. The legs had small rubber grips on the bottom which stopped it sliding around on the floor. It was the best ottoman he had ever used. Montessori noted this with no surprise, only a slight, dizzy nausea. His younger son kept coming into the room to make sure he was comfortable. Bringing him glasses of water, a cookie, and even a beer, which Mrs. Montessori had sent him in with. She stood in the doorway smiling and Montessori raised the bottle to her in salute. He stayed on the couch, with his legs extended, for most of the afternoon. The windows were open. A cool, grass-smelling breeze blew in. He heard his sons playing around in the field behind the house and he heard his wife turning the pages of a magazine in the kitchen. An urge overtook him. Just relax, close his eyes, let his legs extend out forever on the ottoman while the fields and streams extended out forever around the house and the sun looked down forever in its golden power on the earth below.

This urge he fought back by biting the inside of his cheek every so often, and by asking his younger son – when the boy ran sweating and grinning into the room to check up once more – if he could have one of the cans of iced coffee in the fridge. He also inhaled, as deeply as he could, the stale damp smell that still came a little bit from the ottoman (its only defect).

At dinner his wife said: I'm glad that thing is working out.

Montessori said: Seriously, it's the best ottoman I've ever had. I can't believe you just found it in a shop.

His wife said: When I saw it in the window, I knew I had to get it for you.

Josep said: Is it also a "Meervermesser"?

A feather touch on Montessori's right hand.

He said: You know, I didn't look.

His younger son ran off to examine the ottoman. He lifted it up to examine the bottom, poked at the folds of the cloth.

He ran back and said: I didn't see anything! But that doesn't mean it's not the same.

Montessori made sure to use the ottoman whenever he happened to be in the living room. His younger son wanted to move it out onto the back deck whenever Montessori read out there, but Josep dissuaded him by pointing out that the ottoman might get damaged. His younger son compensated by being even more attentive to Montessori's needs, bringing him water, clumsy sandwiches, and even clean socks once "just in case he wanted to change."

This use of the ottoman clearly made Mrs. Montessori very happy. Montessori caught her smiling modestly whenever he sat down and stretched out his legs. He knew that, when they returned, the same expectations would apply. He would sit on the sofa, use the ottoman, read, read, and read, and inhale the (slight) stale damp smell. If Montessori tried to envision this more specifically, his hand tingled a little. If he tried to imagine (for example) putting the ottoman and sofa in the basement, it got stronger. Wherever he went in the house, the ottoman was with him. Certainly when he sat there and read, legs firmly in place and eyes open. Also when he was showering, cutting up meat in the kitchen, taking a shit. The little smell too. It came and it went, but even when it was not there, it left behind the expectation of being smelled.

Two days after the ottoman arrived. Montessori was having trouble sleeping. He had spent the day swimming with his wife and sons, and everyone else had tired themselves out. Not Montessori. He decided to go drink a whiskey and look at the stars. In the kitchen he poured himself a large glass and carried it through the dark living room. Midway across, he stumbled and fell. Some round, softish, even plumpish object had tangled up his legs. The whiskey splashed his clothes, his hair, got into his eyes and made them tear up, and he hit his right shoulder hard. He got to his feet and listened. At least he had not woken anyone else up. He turned on the living room light and saw that the ottoman was pushed far out of its usual position near his spot on the couch, right in the middle of the rug. There was no way his younger son or Josep was responsible. They had gone directly from the pool into the dining room and from the dining room to bed. His wife had gone up only a short while after them. Montessori moved the ottoman back and sat on the couch with his legs extended. He sipped the last few droplets of scotch in the glass and waited until his shoulder began to hurt less. Then he went up to bed.

The next morning his younger son woke him up by poking him in the shoulder.

He said: Can we camp out tonight?

Montessori said: We didn't bring a tent.

His younger son said: That's OK, we can sleep under a tree.

Montessori said: You know, that's a nice idea but maybe we can do it another time.

His younger son said: Please, papa? I've never done it before.

Montessori was about to say no. His hand twinged a little.

He said: Let's see how everyone feels about it. I can't make any promises.

At breakfast, his younger son said: Yeah, and papa said we could camp out.

Montessori said: No, I said we could think about it.

His younger son said: That's still pretty close to what I said.

Mrs. Montessori said: I think it would be a good idea. Not for me personally. I regard camping as an insult to civilization. In general.

Josep said: I agree.

Montessori said: I don't even know if it's legal.

Mrs. Montessori said: It's not like the cops are going to come. Who'd call them?

Their younger son said: It would be so cool.

Montessori said: We don't even have a tent.

A stale smell. A faint smell. It was drifting in, just gently drifting. Montessori got up from his chair. He was sweating, his hands twitching. He felt acid rising in his esophagus, and the shitty pseudoasphyxia this causes.

His younger son said: Other people do it. Other people do it all the time, I bet.

Mrs. Montessori was looking at him. Gaze steady and flat.

She said: Even if you can't camp out, why not go on a hike?

Josep said: Yeah, dad, that's like a solid compromise.

To Montessori's surprise, his younger son smiled in assent.

He said: I am already packed, basically.

His younger son ran off upstairs and came back carrying an open backpack. A blanket was trailing from it. Montessori checked: His younger son had brought the blanket and a flash-light. Montessori lifted it up and clicked the switch. The bulb glowed in a weak, daylight way.

His younger son said: What if we get tired and need to rest on the way? What if there's a cave?

His wife had another work call, so she would not be able to go on the hike. Josep said he'd rather go swimming. There was a book of trail routes provided along with the house. The rental people had mentioned it in their emails. One route, which the book described as easy to intermediate, led up to the top of a smallish mountain from which they could look down into the river valley. It would take most of the day. Despite being a simple ascent (per the book) it was a long one. They would need to pack food, bring water bottles. After breakfast, Montessori loaded his own bag: sandwiches, peanuts, apples, and water bottles. He said goodbye to his wife and Josep, and walked out into the woods with his younger son.

The path began not far from the property edge, according to a handwritten note in the route book's margins, and they found it without any effort. Hikers used it enough that the earth was visible beneath the grass and leaf litter, and two faded ribbons – they looked like they had once been green and yellow – drooped from the overhanging branch of a turkey oak. They walked in silence up the trail. It ascended in long, gentle switchbacks. Montessori held his son's hand. Not too tightly, but he kept it locked in his own. The boy looked up at him, smiling from time to time. He occasionally slipped away to pick up a rock or a twig from the path. He even ran ahead, but Montessori adjusted his own pace at once to keep close to him. When the boy needed to piss, Montessori came and stood with him. His younger son whistled a little and his light stream of urine made a musical rustle against the rocks and leaves.

They reached the summit shortly after noon. To Montessori's surprise the boy was not at all tired. He sat on the flat rock the trail route book had described and ate one of the sandwiches Montessori had fixed. There was a little stream trickling out from a deep, blue-dark cave at the summit. Too small to be entered by anything except a raccoon or something similar, Montessori noted. The water was fresh, clean, very cold. It had the sweet taste of water that has passed through stone. His younger son got down on hands and knees and shone his flashlight into the stream cave. He looked and looked, shrugged like he had not seen anything. He began to drink the stream water. He bent down to the little stream to lap it up, almost like a cat or dog. Montessori sat near him and rested a hand on his warm, slender back as he drank. Montessori drank by lifting the water to his mouth with his right hand.

The summit spread out into a small mesa, and the slope leading down were all as gentle as those on the face they had ascended. Montessori's younger son ran back and forth on the mesa, clambering over the upthrust stones, and he and Montessori developed a game called "stone catch" (his son came up with the name). They tossed rocks off the edge of the mesa and timed how long it took them to roll down out of sight. By the end of it both Montessori and his younger son were hoarse from calling out and cheering. Some of the rocks his younger son picked were slow to move. They moved with a glacial pomposity that amused both Montessori and his son. The sky was serene, cloudless, blank blue. His younger son yelled and yelled words and phrases into the open air so that he could hear them echo down among the pines and the stones of the south-face slopes.

Montessori said: You still want to camp out?

His younger son said: No, let's go back.

Montessori smiled. No pain, not even a twinge.

According to the trail route book, the path down followed the south-facing slopes. It would leave them in a clearing near the footpath along the highway, about two miles from the rental house. They went down together not saying much. Montessori felt happy. His younger son's hand was in his, warm and damp, the bones of the fingers thin and frail-feeling. The path was easy: from one flat outcropping to the next, with short, gentle earth patches in between. His younger son was getting tired, so they stopped to rest from time to time. The sky got cloudier and darker, and an east wind kicked up. It began to smell like rain, and soon a few drops began to fall. Gentle, fat, round droplets. Montessori's younger son tried to catch them in his mouth.

He said: It's good we're not camping out.

Montessori said: Yes, it can be unpleasant in the rain.

The boy was still dashing back and forth to catch the droplets. Montessori's back was beginning to ache. He set himself and massaged his lumbar muscles. He shut his eyes and let the cold rain hit him. He heard his son say: look, papa, come on!

He opened his eyes and saw his son running ahead a little. He was obscured by a large plinth. Montessori ran to catch up, slipping a little on the wet rock. He had to recover himself. When he got to the other side of the plinth, he could no longer see his son.

At first he stood there and shouted the boy's name. In higher and higher tones. *Come on out, come on out. This isn't funny.* All he heard in response was the plopping of the rain and the hard echoes. He began to run back and forth along the outcroppings, calling and calling. He did not see or hear his son. Finally he screamed a loud profanity, because he could think of nothing else to do, then slumped down against the rock wall. His face felt numb, his hands felt numb, his feet, numbness raced up along his spine. He was shaking, as if with fever. He tracked his path back up several hundred yards. He called out his younger son's name again and again. The name spattered against the rocks and broke apart in the air. He peered down the slope. If the boy had fallen, then there would be some sign of him. Or so Montessori believed. He saw no evidence of the boy having fallen down from the post where he had vanished. He had to make sure. He clambered back down. The shaking made it hard. He was feeling more and more nauseated with every movement. He reached the plinth his son had disappeared behind. He saw nothing, no shoe, no jacket, no backpack. He lay flat on the large outcropping behind the plinth and dragged himself forward, hanging out as far over the edge as he dared. He could look straight down. The slope became gentler and gentler as it leveled off into the woods at the base. Still he saw nothing. He screamed and screamed into empty air. He then began to check the slopes directly under the spot where his son had disappeared. There were shrubs and bushes, and a shallow depression covered with underbrush, but he saw no sign of the boy. He had gotten more hoarse from screaming out the boy's name. What should he do now? He found he kept pulling his phone out of his pocket with the intention of calling the police. Every time he saw that he had no service his nausea got worse. Should he go farther down? The boy must have fallen, there was no other possibility. Which meant if Montessori got to him soon enough, then he'd be able to help him. Or had the boy decided to climb back up? He might have gotten sick of the hike and decided to go back on his own. Or he might have gotten distracted by something higher up on the slope and gone to investigate. Montessori's cold hands closed and unclosed. There was no clear way to decide. He had to choose. He chose to keep going down, to keep going down and looking for his son (he refused to permit himself to think *my son's body*). As he was preparing to descend along a slightly different route, he heard a stifled chuckle.

He called out: Is that you? Is that you?

He heard his younger son say: Geez, papa, you shouldn't yell like that, you could get in trouble.

He looked up and saw the boy standing on top of the rock wall he was leaning against. No harm, no visible change. He felt a sick relief pour over him. His younger son had a worried smile on his face. He clambered up and knelt down and put his arms around the boy. He was still shaking.

His younger son said: I thought you would be mad.

Montessori said: No, no, I just got worried because I couldn't see you. It's scary, right?

His younger son said: I was scared too, I wanted to call out but I didn't. I don't know why.

Montessori said: That's OK. That's OK.

Montessori was shaking less. His younger son patted his back.

His younger son said: Are you cold?

The rain got thicker and harder. They moved along, hand in hand again. The rest of the slope down was not hard, but the rain made it slicker so they moved more slowly than otherwise. By the time they reached level ground, they were both soaked. Montessori's younger son had to keep pushing his soaked hair out of his eyes. The rain was so hard now that Montessori wanted to find shelter. There was a rock outcropping that jutted over the bottom of the slope, forming a shallow hollow. He and his younger son walked under the stone and stood there. Water sheeted down past the edges, glassy, cold. Montessori held his son's hand and the boy stuck his free arm through the water sheets.

He said: This is so cool, papa, I'm glad we did this.

There was a flat rock under the outcropping too. Montessori sat his younger son down on it and handed him the water bottle and a small bag of peanuts. The boy ate and drank while Montessori filled his own bottle up by holding it under the rain. The downpour ended. The rain left the air was cool. The path back was simple as well, although the rain had muddied the clear markings Montessori had seen on the way up. He and his son walked on the spongy earth. The boy whistled a little tune and skipped. Montessori made sure to keep him in sight at all times and to hold his hand whenever possible. He kept waiting for a tingling in his right hand. None came.

After they had walked for more than an hour, following the route marked out on the book as well as he could given the recent rain, Montessori realized that he was lost.

He tried to check his phone to see where they were on a map. Highways and other roads cut through the woods, he knew, and if they were close to one he could likely call a car or the state police and explain his situation. There was no service on his phone, none at all. He knew that they needed to be heading roughly southeast, but the sun was hidden so there was no hope of even trying to use it as a compass (not that Montessori rated himself high on such matters, but it would have been better than nothing). Worse still, it was beginning to get dark. The ascent and descent must have taken them much longer than he had realized.

His son, too, was beginning to worry. He had not said anything, but Montessori could tell from the set of his face that he was frightened and tired. At the next set of rocks, Montessori sat down and his son sat next to him and leaned against him. He gave the boy another of the packs of peanuts they had brought with them. He still had three sandwiches, two more bags of peanuts, and four apples.

His younger son said: Papa, are we lost?

Montessori said: I think we got a little turned around, yes.

His younger son said: So then can we camp out?

Montessori said: Let's see.

What about retracing their steps to the south-facing slopes? That was likely the best option. There had been cell reception on the summit. From there he could call his wife, call the state cops, the park service. Or if his younger son had enough energy, they could go back over the north face. Given the approaching dusk and the condition of the trail, this seemed like a bad idea. Stumbling around in the woods in the darkness might lead to injury, animal attack. Yes, he had his son's flashlight. But who knows how long the batteries might last? There was, Montessori saw, a pine stand not far from the rock they were sitting on. The pines grew close together; he found, as he led his son there, a dry hollow under the branches of the largest. The forest floor was covered with dry, soft, shed needles.

Montessori said: You know, I think we are going to camp out.

His younger son said: Wow, can we have a fire?

Montessori said: No, sorry – it's illegal, remember.

His younger son said: Aw, man.

There was a stump at the edge of the pine stand and Montessori set out a small meal on it. A sandwich for his son and a pack of peanuts for himself. It was dark, not cold. There was a kicking, whining breeze. His son's lower lip trembled a little and Montessori took him on his lap.

He said: Don't worry, don't worry.

His son said: I know I wanted to camp out but now I'm scared. What if someone comes and gets me?

Montessori said: I am going to stay awake and keep watch.

He rocked his son. The darkness thickened. He laid out the blanket on the pine needles and covered the boy with his own coat. He still had on a sweatshirt underneath. A fat, white moon came out. The sky was clear again, blank and purplish. Stars pricked out everywhere, more than Montessori had seen in a long time. His son stared up at them too, smiling and smiling. Montessori kept the boy's hand in his. Soon it went slack. His son's eyes closed. It was getting colder, but the hand in Montessori's stayed warm. The white moon looked down with a cool, clerical gaze. Montessori was also tired. There was room under the pine tree for him as well. He kept eyeing the extra space on the warm, dry needles. His back hurt from sitting up against the tree trunk. His legs were starting to go numb. Not from the cold but from the awkward position. He closed his eyes. As he did so, he felt his son's hand slip from his grasp. He opened his eyes at once, sick with panic. The boy was still there, he had just shifted position. Montessori took up the warm slack hand again.

After that, every time he felt sleep beginning to settle on him, he slapped himself hard in the face, or bit his cheek. He bit deeply enough that he could taste a little blood, and that helped keep him awake as well. He should never have quit smoking. That thought came to him again and again. Each time he slapped his own cheek, each time he bit down. He never had any trouble staying awake when he smoked. And think, just think of the lighter's friendly orange flame and the deeper orange glow of the coal.

The boy slept, as far as Montessori could tell, comfortably. He checked his cheek every few minutes to make sure he was staying warm. His small hand stayed warm. It was already past midnight; the sun would rise in less than six hours. Montessori bit and bit the inside of his own cheek harder and harder. He had to switch sides, because the place he bit on the left began to lose feeling. The forest was noisy. It's a lie that forests are quiet at night. Montessori heard the endless, syncopated stridulation of the crickets. Branches sang above him, or the wind sang in them. Some more nightjars (or another kind of bird) gave liquid cries. There was also an intermittent noise, a musical rustle. It was hard for Montessori to isolate, at first. Because it came again and again, eventually he did. A brief sound, a hissing, melodic sound mixed with something that almost resembled a guitar string being strummed. It only occurred at long intervals, and the silence in between also existed separately from the forest noises.

Montessori was preparing to strike himself once more, when he realized what the noise was.

The sound of the first-floor toilet in his house flushing.

He lifted his younger son in his arms. The boy was warm, warm all over, and heavier than Montessori remembered. He did not wake as Montessori lifted him. He dropped his head against Montessori's neck. His warm breath came against Montessori's skin in a gentle plume. He tried to navigate by the moon. He knew he was generally heading southeast, but the forest path was circuitous. It might be taking him far away from the base of the small mountain. It might be a correct circumnavigation. He checked his phone to use the compass a few times. The map application was not working. There was still no service. The land was flat. He had reached a lower elevation and was no longer ascending or descending. His son got heavier and heavier as Montessori walked. The boy was limber and warm. He slumped against Montessori as he had when he was a baby. The musical rustle was getting louder and louder. It came from the trees, from the leaves, from the sky, from the earth. At least that's how it sounded. It was quiet, so quiet. That's why it was so loud. Even the moon with its white shine like the dead spot of light on a lens – even that was rustling away, musically. Montessori's legs and back ached. He kept stumbling over roots and stones sticking up out of the ground. Every time he stumbled, he felt his son slipping out of his grasp and he tightened his arms. Montessori found his own breath was coming shallow and fast. His face was tense and hot, as in childhood. He wanted to stop, only for a minute. The musical rustle could not be all that bad.

Look: there was a stump, nice and flat, with the dead light of the moon shining over the rain-silvered wood. Let's sit there, let's sit there. (Tell me you don't agree).

He stopped, he stopped and stared. His thighs ached and burned. Just sit there, Montessori. No need to torture yourself over these chimerical experiences. The top of the stump was fully whitened by the moon. Like a round, plump eye.

Montessori's younger son snorted a little. Another plume of warm breath. Montessori walked on. His feet were starting to go numb. A twitching pain rose up his spinal column. The musical rustle got louder and louder. His head began to hurt. He felt his pulse thudding at his temples along with the oily, endlessly fluent rush of his blood. Ahead, through the trees, Montessori saw molten white flashes. The musical rustle seemed to rise up most strongly from these. The trees were thinning out. Through the gaps, Montessori saw the sky. Purple, not black. There was a pink, pearly tinge right ahead. The sun was coming up. The molten glints were the vanishing gleams on the chop of a river. He soon exited the forest fully. The river was loud. Up close? No musical rustle at all. The bank was sandy and broad. Pale grayish-blue. No white gleams at all. He carried the boy over to it and sat down with his son in his lap. The boy was starting to wake up. He shifted around, then sat upright.

He said: Are you awake, papa?

The boy's hand touched his face. Montessori said nothing. He tried to smile. He noticed a dark, stumpy shadow near the water edge. Not plump, not round. Upright and square. Taking his son's hand he walked over to it. It was a sign. The green sign of the park service.

It said: THE STATE PARK SERVICE WELCOMES YOU TO MAURERHOLZ BANKS.

There was other writing beneath this. Montessori's vision was too fucked up to make it out in the bad light. His son was picking around in the sandy earth. He lifted up a round, grayish-blue stone. The surface perfect, smooth. He pressed it into Montessori's hand.

Montessori said: Thank you, thank you.

His younger son said: You're welcome, it's a nice rock, right?

There was cell service on the shingle. He called his wife, who did not answer. He left a voicemail explaining where he was. He called the number listed for park service emergencies on the sign. The sun had risen enough for him to read the rest of it.

A man's voice said: Hello, what's your emergency?

Montessori said: My son and I, we're on Maurerholz Banks. We're lost.

The man said: Don't move. Is there a numbered signpost anywhere near you?

Montessori ran to the sign. Painted on the post itself, in gray letters, was MARKER 17.

He gave the man the number. The man said: thank you, we will be there as soon as we can. Don't move. Whatever you do, don't move.

His younger son fell asleep again as they waited. Montessori sat with his hand on the boy's rising and falling chest. The sun came up more and more and the sky became blue. The same empty blue. Dragonflies darted around, their wings clattering. Montessori ate a bag of peanuts. From the south, he saw a wide boat coming up the river toward them. The motor noise woke up his younger son. The boy was rubbing his eyes again and again. Montessori gave him the water flask. The boat came closer and closer. The driver, wearing the green, short pants of the park service, drove it up onto the sandy earth of the shingle and tied its mooring rope to the signpost.

Montessori recognized the boat driver. He had a large mole near his mouth that resembled a fly. Bristly, as if iridescent.

He seemed to recognize Montessori as well. He rubbed his high forehead under his cap.

He said: Are you the one who called?

Montessori said: Yes.

The boat driver said: This happens more than you would think.

He helped Montessori and his younger son onto the wide back of the boat and handed them life vests.

He said: even working as a real estate sign manager isn't enough these days. You see, Mr. Montessori. You see!

He started the engine. They moved with the current. The river was calm. Montessori held his younger son's hand. The boy kept turning around to look out behind the stern at the wide, blue-gray wake. They passed into a narrows, with the sandy banks getting shallower and stonier. Montessori saw they were coming to a bridge. A green sign hung from the side: HARRISON

MEMORIAL PARKWAY. As he read the words: nothing! Not a fucking thing! No feather, no gaze. The boat driver turned back from the helm for a moment and looked right into Montessori's eyes. They were already passing through the somnolent, silent shadow of the bridge. The cold air refreshed Montessori. Downstream of the bridge, not far, they came to a dock. It extended from another shingle, gray and stony. Near where the bank rose up into a blackish cliff, there was a squat building made of brown brick next to a small parking lot and an access path up to the highway that ran alongside the bank. Montessori realized they were not far from the corporate campus where he had first met the boat driver. That was more than a hundred miles (in Montessori's rough estimate) from where the rental was.

The boat driver moored and took them into the squat building. It was cool and cheery inside. It smelled like fresh coffee. There were two couches, deep green. An armchair and a desk with a computer and two telephones. There was a fridge, as well. The boat driver took out a bottle of juice and handed it to Montessori's younger son. He drank it and then curled up on the longer couch.

The boat driver said: We already notified your wife. The service put out an all-points bulletin on you based on her call. She should be here in the next hour or so. When my supervisors spoke to her, she was just leaving.

The small, soft sound of the boy's breathing filled the bright, cool room. Montessori sat down on the smaller couch. His legs hurt, hurt badly. His knees felt swollen and so did his feet. His back sang whenever he tried to move too swiftly.

The boat driver said: Seems like you came a long way. Your wife told my supervisor you were up near Plataea.

Montessori said: How long?

The boat driver shrugged.

He said: You should have some coffee. I'd offer you a cigarette, too, but I quit a while back.

Montessori said: So did I.

The coffee was strong and fresh. It woke Montessori up even more. The boat driver had a cup as well, and sat in the armchair. For a long time he said nothing. Montessori listened to his son's peaceful breathing, the susurration of the river, and the hiss of the infrequent cars on the highway. The boat driver seemed to be considering. He turned his coffee mug around and around in his hands and clenched his jaw.

He said: You still have that mallet I gave you?

Montessori said: Yes, I do. It's in my basement. Safe and sound.

The boat driver said: Is it?

Montessori said: Yes.

The boat driver said: Good. The real estate sign management company will need it back.

Montessori said: When?

The boat driver said: Not just yet.

Montessori's wife arrived an hour later. She was wearing the same clothes she'd been in when he left for the hike. Josep was too. Their faces pale, the eyes bloated. Mrs. Montessori grabbed their younger son first.

The boy said: Hey mama, we got to camp out.

The boat driver tipped his green cap to Montessori and left the park service house. Josep was hugging Montessori, harder than he had since he was his brother's age.

Josep said: Fuck, dad, we were so worried. Sorry for saying fuck.

Montessori said: It's okay.

He poured Mrs. Montessori her own cup of coffee. She sat with the boy as she drank it. Josep had some as well, though he added a lot of milk and sugar. He still grimaced as he swallowed.

Mrs. Montessori said: How did you get all the way down here? It's not possible. I don't understand.

Montessori said: I must have taken a shortcut.

His wife started to laugh. She slapped a hand over her mouth, let it fall.

Montessori said: I need to go talk to the park service guy. Hang on.

His wife and Josep were totally occupied with the boy, stroking his hair and chattering to him. He passed the table where she had set down her purse and quickly dipped his hand in. The car keys were in the change pocket, where she always kept them. He took them without anyone noticing. Outside, he spotted the boat driver at the top of the access path. Montessori walked up to join him. His car was the only one in the lot. He opened the door and climbed in. As he started the engine the boat driver caught his eyes. Before Montessori backed out of the lot, he gave a curt nod.

He turned off his phone before he reached the highway. He knew that his wife would be calling him. The trip back took much less time than the trip out; there was almost no traffic. Not even when he reached the bridge. He expected to become more and more tired as he drove, but he did not. The FOR SALE sign was gone from the yard of Señor Periander's house when he pulled into his own driveway. White curtains covered all the windows. Thick white curtains, nothing could be seen through them. Not even a hat or a mustache. Montessori stayed in his car for a long time. His house stood as it had when he left. One light, upstairs, was on, in Josep's room. He must have forgotten to shut it off before departure.

Music crept out of the house next door. Something German-sounding, lacquered-up chords as if played by a syphilitic giant. Montessori sat and listened for a while before getting out of the car. As soon as he set foot across his property line, a slight sensation tickled his right hand. He kept walking, however. The sensation continued as such until he reached his door and took out his keys. It rose up to a dull near-pain. He ignored it and walked into his house: The pain was banishing the last exhaustion from his body. It increased steadily as he walked down into the basement. Each step, more pain. As he reached the bottom his hand was singing. The mallet was there on the shelf where he had left it. The pain was serious enough that it made it hard to grasp the mallet handle, which was cold and a little greasy. Montessori forced his hand shut and went back up the stairs.

The faint smell. The stale damp smell. It crept into his nose as the music, the syphilitic music, crept into his ears. Whoever had been playing the piece started again, louder this time. The pain in his hand was intense and sickening. It was as bad as the pain that had sent him to the hospital. The edges of his vision dimmed and blurred as he entered the living room. He found that all traces of his exhaustion had vanished as another great wave of pain arrived as he came close to the sofa. So deep and full he almost fell, his knees unlocked. He leaned against the wall to steady himself. The mallet slipped from his right hand and as he knelt to retrieve it, he fell. The smell was thick and heavy. The music was thick and heavy. He was on the ground, bracing himself with his left arm. He was close to vomiting from the pain. Slick, wide saliva filled his mouth. The sofa sat on, in stinking calm. Yellow and green. The late morning light dappled it. Montessori found he was laughing. Quite hard. Spittle dripped from his mouth and acid made his esophagus ache. Dense sweat covered his forehead and his right hand throbbed. He was laughing, really laughing. Simple, clear, clean laughter. He got up, ignored the pain in his hand, raised the mallet high above his head and brought it down on the sofa's right arm. A sharp crack within the frame. The pain got worse. He was still laughing. He had to use his left hand to help his right hand. As you might lift an ax. He lifted the mallet again and brought it down, in the same place. This time the frank broke enough to tear the fabric. The arm dented, a strut of pale wood came through. Along with the deepest, richest, smell he had smelled. He fought back the urge to vomit and struck again. The left arm. The scrollwork along the back. The front edge under the cushion. The music next door was getting louder and louder. The smell here was getting richer and deeper. His clothes were drenched and more spit leaked from his mouth. He raised the mallet and brought it down. Raised the mallet and brought it down. Raised the mallet and brought it down. Raised the mallet and brought it down. Raised the mallet and brought it down.

The sofa's left front leg splintered. So did the right, after two more blows. This piece of shit, this eternal piece of shit was now kneeling. Thought Montessori. He struck five more blows. Seven. The left rear leg splintered and then the right. His hand was passed through. No other word for it. Passed through. Passed through and passed through. Do you know it? You must know it. Not pain but what lies beyond pain. He hit the sofa again. Across the bowed wooden arch with its scroll, along the back. It broke at a central point. The music stopped. All at once. The smell stopped. All at once. The pain stopped. All at once.

Montessori stood there panting a little. His clothes stuck to him. The sofa was on the ground, splayed out. The broken wooden struts had torn through the cushion and cloth. A dead sofa. A fucking dead sofa. The mallet was light and easy in his hand. He was thirsty, he found. He walked to the kitchen and turned on the faucet. He drank from the faucet. The cool, sweet water soothed his throat and esophagus.

While he was drinking, he heard a little noise. Not a musical rustle; hardly anything. He entered the first-floor bathroom. The faucet handle was lightly veiled with frost and the toilet was trying to play its little flute. He broke the sink with three blows. The porcelain cracked and it came off the wall. Water began to leak from the pipes, but he knelt down and shut it off. He smashed apart the toilet tank as well. That took only two blows. A lot of water came out, but it stopped after he closed off the valve against the wall. Broken porcelain covered the bathroom floor. He broke the mirror. One blow. Slivered glass fell on top, with almost no sound at all.

The upstairs mirrors also took no time to break. Each one, one blow. So much for the cool, clerical gaze. There was no sound, no music, from the house next door.

He walked back downstairs. He wanted to go sit outside. He stopped in the living room to admire the dead sofa again. Once he got into the backyard, he remembered: the cat collar tag. It was still there and still staring at him. The last cool clerical gaze. For this he did not need his mallet. He lifted it up off the cross and scraped a shallow hole next to where Old Abel lay in the lawn. He put the collar back in and covered it up with dirt. He sat in the Adirondack chair and turned on his phone. He had missed dozens of text messages from his wife, as well as 11 voicemails. He did not answer these. He called the number of the furniture store they liked.

The sales representative said: Hello, how may I help you?

Montessori said: Hello, my name is Montessori. I had ordered a couch from you but it was on back order and I wanted to check in and see what the wait was looking like.

The representative said: How do you spell the last name?

Montessori spelled it. The line went silent briefly. The representative came back.

She said: I have good news, Mr. Montessori. It's available now. Would you like to arrange delivery?

Montessori said: What is the fastest I can get it?

The representative said: We can have it to you today by 8PM, if you're willing to pay the expedited delivery charges.

Montessori said: I am willing.

After they had finalized the purchase and delivery, Montessori lay in the Adirondack chair. The morning was warm but not hot. A stiff, uneven breeze blew over him. He'd need to speak to his wife. She would be angry. She would not believe him. He might have to go to counseling. She might even leave, or demand that he leave. He had wrecked the house, ruined a valuable antique. She'd have every right to demand such a thing. For the moment, Montessori let the air, sky, and clouds flow over him. The earth he had scraped up was still cool under his nails. Though his back and arms were slightly sore from his exertions, he felt no pain.

His wife was texting him again. Please, please said the texts. Please let us know you're alright. Montessori started to write back but he did not at first. He did not know what to say. If he told her he was alright, then when she eventually came home she'd think he had really gone crazy. If he said nothing, she would only grow more and more frantic. Are you at the house, said the text. Montessori wrote back. Yes, and a thumbs-up symbol. It seemed even stupider than usual. He picked up the mallet – which seemed much, much lighter – and carried it upstairs to his bedroom. It was cool and quiet in there. The mirror shards reflected the white, empty ceiling. Montessori thought about cleaning them up but decided he would do it later. Right now, he needed a nap. His wife would be there in three hours at most, and he had to be well-rested when she arrived. Otherwise, he would never be able to explain.

And precisely, precisely because it was so trivial. A smashed-up sofa, a smashed-up bathroom. Seven broken mirrors. The damage to the bathroom would cost them several thousand to fix. They had the money. They had more than enough. Now that the transactional phase was completed, they'd have still more. What was he supposed to say? He could try blaming it on his hand wound. Though he'd been officially cured of that. Perhaps there was some lingering effect from chimerical experiences he could appeal to. He could say nothing. Shrug a few times, apologize. See what happened.

The mallet made a shallow dimple in the bed next to him. The head was black rubber, deep black. With the chemical, comforting smell of vulcanized rubber. The handle was smooth, cool now. Light, light. He closed his eyes. He listened to the silence from the street. From the house next door. From his own house. He fell asleep in the cool bed with his hand around the cool handle of the mallet. He dreamed though his dreams remained obscure to him at each moment. He knew he was dreaming. The sleep was perfect. So deep and perfect. He could have gone on sleeping forever had it not been for the little pipe piping. At first, he was frightened. Because this might be the mustache too. But not: it was high, shrill. Not like the mustache at all. The piping got bigger and bigger, wider and wider. An open and opening throat. He woke up. Someone was yelling and shrieking. Downstairs. He knew the voice. It was his wife. He grabbed the mallet and ran. As he reached the stair bottom, he stopped. He saw the living room. His wife stood by the door. She was yelling. His younger son was wrapped in Josep's arms, head pressed against his brother's shoulder. Both boys were kneeling. Josep's eyes and open mouth quivered.

On the floor, where the wreckage of the sofa had been, lay something else.

Roundish and plumpish. Wearing a green suit. A yellow necktie (the body was turned on its side). Its arms and legs were visibly broken, as was its ribcage. The face was smashed beyond recognition, and a huge divot lay open in the skull. Gray, pearly gray and pink. A red-brown pool spread around the body. A smell thick in the air. Rich and coppery. In the room's corner, a bowler hat and spectacles. The spectacles were broken. Mrs. Montessori saw her husband. She stopped screaming and covered her open mouth with her hand. Josep's cheeks turned gray. He was blinking, blinking, blinking.

Mrs. Montessori said: I thought it was you! For a second I thought it was you!

Montessori was going to answer (I swear it). But the laughter took all his words.

SAM MUNSON is the author of *Dog Symphony* (New Directions), *The War Against the Assholes* (Saga), and *The November Criminals* (Doubleday). His fiction has appeared in *Granta*, *Guernica*, *McSweeney's*, *n+1*, *Tablet*, and elsewhere.

UNCORRECTED ADVANCE PROOF

Pub date: November 11, 2025
Genre: Fiction
Print ISBN: 9781953387974 | Price: $17.95 US
Digital ISBN: 9781953387967 | Price: $9.99 US
Format: Paperback (Gatefold)
Size: 5.5 x 7.5 in.

Publicity Contact:
Brett Gregory, brett@twodollarradio.com

DISTRIBUTED TO THE TRADE BY:
Publishers Group West
1700 Fourth St., Berkeley, CA 94710
pgw.com | phone 510-809-3700 | orders 800-283-3572

Please do not quote without
a comparison with the finished book.

Indie Next List Nominations
(ABA member booksellers)

*November 2025 titles have a deadline of
August 25, 2025*